**Come on, Wonder.
Win this one for the Griffens . . .**

Behind Wonder on the outside Charad was rapidly
gaining, and the two fillies were leaving the rest of the
field behind. Wonder held on to the half-length lead,
but the pace was blazing. They'd run the first half-
mile in close to track-record time. Ashleigh held her
breath as the horses pounded down the backstretch.
At this rate, Wonder would use up everything before
she even got into the final stretch.

Ashleigh heard Charlie mumble, "Hold her till the
turn. Don't let that filly pressure you!"

"Will Wonder have anything left?" Ashleigh asked
Charlie anxiously.

"She should. We'll see."

The crowd in the grandstands was going wild. Wonder and Charad came off the turn with Wonder barely
a half-length in the lead. Charad's jockey went for his
whip.

"Now!" Charlie barked. "Let her out!"

Ashleigh saw Jilly do just that. She loosened the
tension on Wonder's reins, leaned down tight over
Wonder's withers, and kneaded her hands along the
filly's neck.

Wonder shot forward.

Collect all the books in the THOROUGHBRED series:

Coming Soon:

Also by Joanna Campbell

And look for:

THOROUGHBRED

WONDER'S FIRST RACE

JOANNA CAMPBELL

HarperPaperbacks

A Division of HarperCollins*Publishers*

HarperPaperbacks   *A Division of* HarperCollins*Publishers*
                    10 East 53rd Street, New York, N.Y. 10022

Produced by Daniel Weiss Associates, Inc.
33 West 17th Street, New York, New York 10011.

First printing: October 1991

Printed in the United States of America

HarperPaperbacks and colophon are trademarks of
HarperCollins*Publishers*

10 9 8 7 6 5

WONDER'S FIRST RACE

"HOLD HER!" CHARLIE BURKE GROWLED TO THE FOURTEEN-year-old girl at his side.

Ashleigh Griffen took a firmer grip on the lead shank of the prancing chestnut Thoroughbred. "Just take it easy, Wonder," she said to the horse. Then she turned to the old man who was trying to tighten the girth on Wonder's saddle. "She can't help being ex-cited, Charlie. Today's her first race. She knows how important it is. Don't you, girl?"

The beautiful filly steadied, then pushed her nose against Ashleigh's shoulder. Ashleigh felt her own ex-citement growing as she gazed around at the commo-tion in the saddling area of Churchill Downs Race-track. She could hardly believe that she and Wonder were finally here. The road to this race had been such a hard one, and Wonder's trials weren't over yet. So much relied on her doing well in her first race.

There were beads of sweat on Ashleigh's forehead, and although she'd pulled back her dark, shoulder-length hair, damp tendrils were already clinging to her cheeks and the back of her neck. If she was feeling the heat, she knew Wonder would be feeling it even more.

The filly's coat gleamed copper in the July sunshine. Her long mane shimmered in a silky wave as she tossed her head and fidgeted on slender, powerful legs.

Charlie finished buckling the girth, checked its tightness with his fingers, and dropped the saddle flap into place. He stepped back a few feet and inspected Wonder, nodding and pushing his rumpled felt hat back on his head. From his baggy cotton shirt and trousers, it would be hard to guess that he was a respected trainer. "She'll do," he said gruffly. He turned to study the other two-year-old fillies being readied on the lush grass by their trainers and grooms. There weren't any big races on the card that hot July afternoon, but there were still plenty of spectators standing around the saddling area. Their voices mingled with those of trainers, grooms, and jockeys preparing to go to the walking ring.

"You should have heard them before we left Townsend Acres this morning," Ashleigh said. Her ears were still ringing with the negative comments of some of the staff at the famous racing stable. "Jennings said to me, 'She's not going to live up to her sire. You and

Charlie are living on daydreams.' " Ashleigh accurately mimicked the assistant trainer's voice.

"What do you expect from Jennings?" Charlie snapped. "He nearly ruined her in her early training with that heavy handling." Charlie brushed his hand across his forehead and looked around. "She's not sweating up like some of them," he said, "but we won't know what they've got till we get out on the track. Where's Jilly?"

No sooner had he spoken than a slim young woman wearing the green-and-yellow racing silks of Townsend Acres rushed across the grass. Her blond hair was braided into a single plait that hung between her shoulders, and she carried her helmet under her arm. At twenty-two, Jilly had been riding as an apprentice jockey for Townsend Acres for almost a year. Today she'd be trying for her first win.

"Sorry I'm late," Jilly said breathlessly. "The other jockeys were kidding me after I weighed in—asking me how I expected to get a green horse around the track without a crop."

"Ignore them," Charlie said. "You know she'll back right off if she so much as sees a crop."

Jilly put on her helmet and adjusted the chin strap. "How do you see the race playing out?" Ashleigh noticed there was a nervous catch in Jilly's voice, but outwardly, Jilly seemed calm.

"The first thing to remember," Charlie said, "is that

3

all of the fillies in this race, except Wonder, have raced before. None of them has won, or they wouldn't be in a maiden race, but they have an edge on her there. They know what it's like to be out in front of a crowd, running in a big field. You're going to have to watch that Wonder doesn't get distracted. Remember this first race is really a testing ground," Charlie added. "Let the filly get her feet wet. It'd be nice to win, but we may not. Just get her to run the best race she can." Charlie glanced up. "Looks like it's time to head to the walking ring. You ready?" he said to Ashleigh.

Ashleigh nodded, but her throat was tight. She'd never done this before, and she was only too aware of the spectators studying the horses as they were led forward. They were looking at pre-race behavior— overexcitement or listlessness that could indicate a horse's chances of winning. Charlie gave Jilly a leg into the saddle. Ashleigh straightened her shoulders and led Wonder forward into the ring.

When Wonder eyed the crowd, she immediately flared her delicate nostrils and snorted. "Just take it easy," Ashleigh said, glancing over to the horse. Wonder's neck was arched, and her ears were pricked. Her hard muscles rippled under her gleaming chestnut coat. Ashleigh knew the filly was as tense about her first pre-race experience as she herself was. Wonder's bright coat was darkening with nervous sweat.

"I know how you feel," Ashleigh whispered soothingly. "But everything's going to be fine. You're going to go out there and show them just how good you are!"

Wonder flicked her ears, listening to Ashleigh's familiar voice, but she was too keyed up to give her full attention. She tossed her head and toe-danced across the grass at the end of the lead shank.

"She'll be okay once we get out there," Jilly assured Ashleigh as the trainers came into the ring. It was time for the horses and jockeys to go to the track.

"Go nice and easy with her up to the gate," Charlie said to Jilly. "Let her get a good look at everything. All set?"

Jilly nodded, picked up the reins, and settled herself in the saddle. "We're going to go out there and win, aren't we girl?" Charlie and Ashleigh both stepped away as Jilly started Wonder forward.

"Good luck!" Ashleigh called. Jilly urged Wonder out of the walking ring. A line of escort riders were waiting, and one of them rode up to Jilly and Wonder.

"Nothing more we can do here," Charlie said as the horses and riders moved off in a line under the grandstand toward the track. Ashleigh shaded her eyes with her hand and looked up into the famous Churchill Downs grandstand, with its twin peaked towers. She saw her seventeen-year-old sister, Caroline, blond and pretty in a bright summer outfit, waving to catch their attention. Brad Townsend was standing beside her.

A frown flickered across Ashleigh's face. It still irked her that her sister was dating the arrogantly handsome son of the owner of Townsend Acres, but it bothered her more that Brad would be watching Wonder's first race. Brad was Wonder's biggest critic. He was training his own two-year-old, Townsend Prince, star of the new crop of racing stock at the farm, and if Wonder didn't do well today, Brad would be right there giving Ashleigh one of his infuriatingly knowing smiles and saying, "I told you so."

Ashleigh tapped Charlie on the arm and pointed to Caroline and Brad. The two of them made their way up the steps. Brad, with his dark hair brushed smoothly in place, was dressed casually in jeans and a designer shirt.

As Ashleigh and Charlie stepped into the row in front, Caroline smiled cheerfully, then leaned down and spoke in Ashleigh's ear. "Vanity Girl and Winsome have been putting in some good breezes. Brad says Wonder will have a tough time against them. And her odds aren't very good. She's up to thirty to one."

"Then the people betting on Wonder will make some money, won't they?" Ashleigh snapped back. Caroline had never had any interest in horses. She was the only member of the Griffen family who didn't. But since she'd started dating Brad, Caroline was talking like she was an expert, mimicking every word Brad said. It completely annoyed Ashleigh.

Behind her, Ashleigh heard Brad chuckle. "Throw away their money is more like it."

Ashleigh deliberately ignored him and riveted her full attention on the track. Wonder seemed calmer as Jilly circled her behind the gate, waiting for their turn to go in. Ashleigh didn't feel the least bit calm.

Finally the last horse was in, and an expectant hush fell over the crowd. Ashleigh glued her eyes to the Number Six post position—Wonder and Jilly. "You can do it, Wonder," she whispered under her breath.

The gate doors flew open, and ten Thoroughbreds surged powerfully out onto the dirt track. Horses and jockeys fought for position. Wonder was off half a beat late, and the horses to either side of her suddenly swerved in together, blocking her path.

Ashleigh cringed and held her breath as Jilly was forced to pull Wonder up and search for another route. Wonder didn't like running behind horses, and being caught in the pack also increased the chances of Wonder seeing a flying whip. And after the bad experiences Wonder had had with whips during her early training, Ashleigh and Charlie had reason to fear Wonder's reaction.

As the field raced along the backstretch, Ashleigh bit her lip, searching for an opening. But Jilly and Wonder were still blocked in the middle of the pack. They had nowhere to go and a lot of ground to make up.

Then one of the horses in front swerved out slightly toward the middle of the track. A narrow opening appeared in front of Wonder. The filly surged through without any urging from Jilly. Jilly moved Wonder out toward the center of the track and started moving up around horses.

"That's it," Charlie cried. "Keep her out there! Don't let her get boxed in again."

The voice of the announcer echoed in Ashleigh's ears. "Vanity Girl and On The Top are fighting for the lead. Marchmaid's dropping out of it, but Winsome's coming between horses to challenge. They're approaching the far turn . . ."

Only a quarter of the six-furlong race was still to be run. Wonder and Jilly were rapidly gaining on the outside, moving up from fifth, to fourth, then into position to challenge the three front-runners. On The Top was tiring. She swayed out across the track, in Wonder's path.

Ashleigh heard Charlie growl, but she was too intently absorbed in the drama of the race to make the slightest sound herself.

The tiring filly swayed further out, leaving a gap between herself and Winsome. Jilly and Wonder shot through.

"Way to go!" Ashleigh shouted. "Come on, Wonder!"

"And here comes Ashleigh's Wonder," the announcer called, "moving up fast on the leader . . . this filly's flying. . . ."

Ashleigh's heart pounded as Wonder surged by Winsome and then began to move up on the front-running Vanity Girl. With each stride, Wonder moved closer to the lead.

The other riders were going for their whips. Jilly had to fight to keep Wonder clear. Then suddenly it didn't matter, because Wonder was in front, racing down the middle of the track. She was clear by a half-length, then a length.

Ashleigh screamed at the top of her lungs, "Go, girl, go! Come on, baby!"

"And Ashleigh's Wonder has the lead," the announcer cried. Ashleigh saw Jilly glance back under her arm, then knead her hands along Wonder's neck, asking the filly for still more speed. Wonder responded. She stretched her long legs, lengthening her stride.

As they approached the wire, Wonder was drawing further away from the field.

"That's my girl!" Ashleigh screamed as Wonder swept under the wire, three lengths in front and still pouring on the speed. "She did it, Charlie! She did it!" In her excitement, she realized she was slapping the old man's shoulder. Charlie didn't mind. He'd pulled off his felt hat and was happily pounding it to a pulp.

When Ashleigh glanced back, she saw that Brad was completely stunned. He kept shaking his head as if he couldn't believe what he'd just seen. *Serves you right,* Ashleigh thought smugly.

2

IT WAS NEARLY DARK WHEN JILLY TURNED THE HORSE VAN INTO
the long drive of Townsend Acres, outside of Lexington. Ashleigh and Charlie sat on the front seat beside
her. During the seventy-five-mile trip, the three of
them had talked nonstop of Wonder's victory and the
new prospects for her future.

In the fading light, the rolling, white-fenced paddocks spreading out endlessly to either side of the
drive looked serene. A few Thoroughbreds grazed on
the rich summer grass, but most of the valuable horses
had been brought into the barns for the night.

Jilly turned left at the fork in the drive and headed
toward the working area of the farm. The oak-lined
fork to the right led up to the Townsends' huge house
at the top of the rise.

They passed the Griffens' house on the right of the
drive and the breeding and foaling barns opposite.

11

Three years before, Ashleigh's parents had come to Townsend Acres as the new breeding managers. They'd been forced to sell their own Thoroughbred breeding farm, Edgardale, after a virus had swept through their stables, killing stock. It had been an absolutely horrible time for all of them, but they'd gradually healed and become involved with their new life —and if they hadn't come to Townsend Acres, Ashleigh reminded herself, she wouldn't have Wonder.

Jilly parked the van in the drive of the sprawling training complex. Surrounding them were the stable buildings, training rings, storage barns, and the live-in staff's quarters, where Jilly and Charlie each had rooms.

As late as it was, grooms were still sitting on the benches outside, enjoying the slightly cooler night air. Several hurried over to the van.

"So, she won," Tom Hart, one of the older grooms, called out to Charlie.

"News travels fast," Charlie said gruffly.

Tom laughed. "The Townsend kid got here a couple of hours ago in that fancy sports car of his. Went right in to check out the Prince."

Charlie was already unlocking the back doors of the van. "Let's get her unloaded," he said to Ashleigh. "She's had a full day . . . deserves a good rest in her stall."

Ashleigh was thinking the same thing. As soon as

the doors were open and the ramp down, she jumped up into the van. Wonder had traveled alone, since she'd been the only Townsend Acres horse to race the last weekend of the Churchill Downs season. The filly whickered happily, glad the journey was over and anxious for her roomy, comfortable stall.

"Yeah, girl, I know," Ashleigh said, rubbing Wonder's head and unclipping her lead shank. "Let's get you out of here." Carefully, she backed Wonder down the ramp and onto the graveled drive. Wonder lifted her head and sent a loud whinny echoing through the stable yard. Several horses inside answered her.

"You telling them how great you did?" Ashleigh said with a laugh. "Come on, let's go." Ashleigh led Wonder toward the huge stable building, and Charlie followed behind.

"After I put the van away, I'm headed for bed," Jilly called out. "I'm beat, and I've got to be up by four. See you guys in the morning."

"Night, Jilly," Ashleigh called. "And thanks for riding such a great race!"

Wonder was delighted to see her stall again. She went straight to her hay net after Ashleigh led her inside.

"None the worse for wear," Charlie said as he quickly checked the filly over. "She came out of the race just fine. I'm off, too. We'll rest her tomorrow, but we'll have plenty of work to do after that. I'll talk to Townsend in the morning about future races."

"Night," Ashleigh said as he shuffled off. Before she went home herself, she filled Wonder's water bucket and hay net, readjusted the light, netted sheet over Wonder's back, then patted the filly's shoulder. "Sleep tight, girl. I'm so proud of you!"

Wonder nickered contentedly as she tore off a mouthful of hay. Ashleigh closed and bolted the stall door, then headed out of the stable and down the drive. The summer air smelled of grass and damp earth, and in the distance crickets sounded their cry. The front light was on, but Ashleigh's parents had already gone to bed. They had to be up at the crack of dawn. Ashleigh tiptoed up the stairs, but surprisingly, Caroline was still awake when Ashleigh went into the bedroom they shared. She was curled up on her bed reading a magazine.

She looked up. "I thought you guys would never get home. Where've you been?"

"It took a while to get Wonder cooled out and ready to go," Ashleigh yawned, digging under her pillow for her pajamas. "And you can't drive a horse van that fast."

"Mmm," Caroline answered. "Brad and I were talking about the race on the way home. He says Wonder may end up making a decent second-grade allowance horse. He's going to talk to his father. He thinks they can probably schedule her for some ungraded races in the fall when the Kentucky tracks reopen—you know, against fillies at her level. And Brad says—"

Ashleigh froze by the side of her bed and glared at her sister. "Wonder just ran a fantastic first race—and won it! I'm not going to listen to Brad putting her down!"

"Six months ago you didn't know if she'd even go to the track. I thought you'd be glad that they definitely want to put her in races," Caroline said indignantly.

"They? Who's they? Now that Charlie and I have done all the work, I suppose Brad wants to butt in? He doesn't even know what he's talking about. Wonder's not a second-grade allowance horse—she's *good* . She's got the speed and heart to run in graded races, with the best horses. Brad just doesn't want to admit he was wrong about her!"

Caroline flipped her magazine closed and sat up in bed. "I know how much you care about Wonder, but you're not being very realistic. At least she's racing. You should be glad about that. And Brad's father does own her, remember."

"Yeah, and he turned Wonder's training over to Charlie and me, because *we* were able to turn her around. *He* thinks we know what we're doing, even if Brad doesn't!"

"Don't get so upset!" Caroline snipped. "I thought you'd be glad to hear what Brad thought."

Ashleigh crushed her pajamas in her hands. "Do me a favor, Caro, and don't mention his name again. I'm really *sick* of hearing it!"

Ashleigh flung across the room and out the door.

In the bathroom, she grabbed her toothbrush from the rack. She was furious. She'd been so excited about Wonder winning her very first race—not many horses did that—but Brad and Caro seemed determined to try and spoil it. Not Caro so much, since she only repeated everything Brad said, like a parrot. But Ashleigh had had all she could take of Brad. She spit a mouthful of toothpaste in the sink and splashed cold water over her hot cheeks, trying to calm down.

Caro's light was out when Ashleigh returned to the bedroom. She climbed right into bed and pulled her covers up to her chin. She was so tired. It was nearly eleven, and she'd been up since three in the morning in order to get to the track on time. She was beginning to feel a little guilty, too. Maybe she shouldn't have lost her temper, but why did Caro have to take Brad's side all the time? And Caro had picked the absolutely worst time to start in. Ashleigh might have been able to ignore it if she hadn't been so exhausted. She closed her eyes. Wonder really was good, no matter what anyone said. The little filly, who'd nearly died at birth, was going places.

* * *

"I can't see why Mr. Townsend's waiting," Ashleigh's best friend, Linda March, said as the two girls sprawled on the grass beside the farm's swimming hole on a sticky August afternoon. "Why doesn't he race Wonder again? You'd think he'd leave it up to Charlie to decide." Linda brushed some blond curls from her eyes. She was as fair as Ashleigh was dark. Both girls were athletic and about the same height—five foot three. They'd been friends since Ashleigh's first day at Henry Clay Middle School.

"Charlie says Mr. Townsend has other things on his mind, like Townsend Prince!" Ashleigh growled. She was frustrated and angry with the way things were going. "Brad's been telling everyone that they'd be wasting their time to race Wonder before the small fall races. None of them think Wonder can go longer distances, or against stiffer competition."

Ashleigh rolled to her side and angrily plucked at some long blades of grass. "Charlie hasn't given up. He's trying to convince Mr. Townsend to enter Wonder in a mile allowance at Pimlico in a couple of weeks."

"I thought everything would be great after she won," Linda sighed.

"So did I." Ashleigh suddenly sat up and called to her nine-year-old brother, who was gradually moving farther and farther downstream on his pony, Moe. "Rory, stay where I can see you."

"Come on, Ash," he called back. He and his pony were soaked, and his reddish gold hair was plastered to his head. "It's no fun if I have to stay here! Moe isn't going to do anything stupid."

"No, but you might. You'll forget all about the time, and then I'll have to come looking for you." Ashleigh glanced at her watch. "Besides, we should be heading back anyway."

Reluctantly, Rory turned his pony and headed back to the girls. Ashleigh and Linda collected the farm's two riding horses—the Appaloosa mare, Belle, and the big bay, a retired race horse named Dominator. Rory trotted up as they mounted, and they all set off between the white-fenced paddocks toward the barns.

Charlie was waiting when they rode into the stable yard. His blue eyes were almost twinkling as he greeted them. "Well," he said to Ashleigh, "I just got some good news. Townsend's finally agreed to the Pimlico race. I can't say he thinks she'll win, but we'll be shipping her up to Maryland a week from Thursday."

"It's about time!" Ashleigh cried. "All right!"

"Now you'll show them," Linda grinned.

3

CAROLINE SAT ON THE EDGE OF HER BED, WATCHING ASHLEIGH
pack. "You're so disorganized, Ashleigh."

Ashleigh barely heard her. Had she remembered her
extra jeans? She dug down in the depths of her duffle
bag and found them, but she'd forgotten her rain
slicker. She ran to the closet, grabbed it off the hanger,
and rolled it up to stuff into her bag.

"You've known for almost two weeks that you were
going to Pimlico," Caroline added. "Why didn't you
pack last night?"

"I hate packing, and then Linda came over, and we
all ended up at Jilly's apartment, talking. Anyway, I
think I've got everything."

"Your hairbrush?" Caro motioned with her head in
the direction of Ashleigh's dresser.

"Oh, right!" Ashleigh dashed over and collected the
brush and a handful of bands for fastening her hair.

"Well, I hope Wonder does real well," Caroline said.

"Thanks!" Ashleigh gave her sister a smile. Caroline had been very careful to avoid any mention of Wonder's progress, or Brad, and Ashleigh was feeling in a generous mood. "Too bad you can't go to Pimlico with Brad."

"Brad'll tell me about it when he gets back. We have a date Saturday night. His father's taking some business people to the race, and there's not enough room in the private plane."

Ashleigh knew Townsend Prince was entered in a stakes race at Pimlico the same day Wonder was running. It was considered a sure thing around the stables that he'd win. Few people had as much confidence in Wonder, but Ashleigh hadn't discussed Wonder's chances with her sister. One look at Caroline's face showed that her sister agreed with the majority.

"Ashleigh!" Rory shouted up the stairs from the front hall. "Jilly's here!"

"Coming!" Ashleigh called back. She thrust her hairbrush into her duffle bag and closed it. If she'd forgotten anything else, it was too late now.

"Have fun," Caroline said.

"I will," Ashleigh answered as she hurried from the bedroom. "See you Sunday night."

Rory and Ashleigh's parents were standing in the hall talking to Jilly as Ashleigh pounded down the stairs.

"I wish I was going with you," Rory groaned. "I never get to do fun stuff like you."

"You will when you're older," Ashleigh said, ruffling her brother's hair.

Mrs. Griffen dropped a kiss on Ashleigh's cheek. "Be careful. Don't go anywhere without Charlie or Jilly."

"Mom!" Ashleigh groaned. "I'm not exactly a baby."

"Sorry," her mother said, smiling sheepishly. "But there are all kinds of characters hanging around racetracks."

"Ashleigh's got a head on her shoulders," Mr. Griffen said. "I won't even tell you to have a good time because I know you will. We'll be cheering for Wonder. Good luck."

"Thanks, Dad." Ashleigh kissed both her parents good-bye, then hurried outside with Jilly.

At eight in the morning the temperature was already close to eighty, and it wouldn't be any cooler in Maryland.

Charlie was waiting in Jilly's pickup truck. Ashleigh threw her duffle bag in the back and climbed in beside him. Wonder, Townsend Prince, and several other horses that would be racing over the weekend had left in one of the farm's big horse vans at dawn.

"Gonna be a long drive," Charlie said. "Haven't taken these old bones on a trip like this for a while."

"I'll bet you're as excited as we are," Jilly teased.

"A track is a track," he muttered, but Ashleigh could see the anticipation on his face.

They were exhausted by the time they arrived at the track, but they were keyed up, too. Jilly parked on the backside of the track near the stabling barns, and they all climbed out, glad to stretch their legs. Charlie would be staying at the track, but Jilly and Ashleigh were sharing a room in a nearby motel.

Charlie grabbed his bag from the bed of the pickup and immediately set out for the stalls that had been reserved for the Townsend Acres' horses. They found Wonder halfway down a long line of stalls, with her head over the door, curiously inspecting her new surroundings. The filly had had an hour or so to relax after her trip, and she looked comfortable. She whinnied eagerly as soon as she saw them.

Ashleigh hurried up to the stall, welcoming Wonder's nuzzled greeting. "Looks like the ride didn't bother you much," Ashleigh said as she rubbed the filly's ears.

"She seems to be in better shape than this old man," Charlie said. He opened the stall door and shooed Wonder back as he stepped inside with Ashleigh behind him. He looked the filly over critically, checking her legs in particular for any cuts or scrapes. Even though Wonder's legs had been carefully bandaged before the trip, horses frequently injured themselves or others by nipping or kicking out in the van. "She looks fine," he said. "One of the grooms got her set for the night. Time you two girls got yourselves to bed, too. Long day tomorrow. I thought maybe I'd let you try breezing her in the morning," he added to Ashleigh.

Ashleigh hadn't even dared ask him if she could have a chance. She'd figured Jilly would do all the exercising at the track. Now all she could do was stare at him.

"Gotta try sometime," Charlie said. "See you two here about five tomorrow."

Charlie was already waiting at Wonder's stall when the girls arrived bright and early the next morning. The sun was barely over the horizon, and the sky was tinged with pink. "I've already groomed and fed her," Charlie told Ashleigh. "There'll be a lot of horses working this morning. I want to get out there early."

Ashleigh nodded. She went into the stall at Wonder's welcoming nicker. "Morning, girl. Looks like you had a good night." She clipped the lead shank to Wonder's halter and led her out of the stall. Charlie already had the tack piled on the grooming trunk outside the stall.

Charlie lifted Wonder's saddle and slid it gently onto the filly's back. At the touch of the saddle, Wonder snorted excitedly. "Looks like she wants to get out there and do a little running." Charlie buckled the girth. "I don't want to push her too much . . . just enough to get her on her toes for the race tomorrow. After she's warmed up, let's gallop her for six furlongs. But nothing too fast. Just enough to work out the kinks. The six furlongs in a minute and a quarter is all I'm looking for. We're not out to impress anybody with her times this morning. Keep her at a jog the first couple of laps till she gets used to the track and the surface. It won't be the same as Churchill Downs or the oval at home. Every track has a slightly different feel and consistency. This track's good and fast. She should take to it fine."

Ashleigh eased the bridle over Wonder's head. The filly took the bit eagerly. "You know what's coming, don't you?" Ashleigh said as she buckled the nose and chin straps and tried to check her own nervous excitement.

Ashleigh led Wonder as Charlie set off purposefully down the barn aisle, past dozens of stalls containing sleek Thoroughbreds, past grooms and exercise riders and trainers moving about the aisle to either side. The early morning activity was more hushed than it would be later in the day before each race, but Ashleigh noticed several people look their way, appraising Wonder.

"They're always curious about new horses," Jilly whispered to Ashleigh. "Especially the two-year-old crop. And if they've been gossiping like they usually do, they already know Wonder's bloodlines and everything about her history. They're sizing her up. Though they're not going to tell much from her workout this morning, since Charlie wants to take it easy."

As they approached the track in the dawn light, Ashleigh saw that several horses were already working, but the dirt surface was still fairly unmarred by hoofprints. Charlie led them to the track opening, then paused to give Ashleigh a leg up into the saddle.

"Relax, missy," he said. "Don't want her catching a case of nerves."

Ashleigh took a deep breath. *This is just another morning workout,* she told herself. *Just like we do every morning at home. Forget that you happen to be riding at a famous track.* She picked up the reins, gathered them firmly, and settled herself in the saddle.

"Keep her out in the center of the track for the jog," Charlie said. "Move her in closer to the rail when I give you the signal. Start galloping her at the three-quarter pole, then come around to the wire. Got it?"

Ashleigh nodded. She felt a small hollow pit in her stomach. She had to do this well. She couldn't make a fool of herself in front of the other, experienced exercise riders. And she had to do her best for Wonder, too.

Charlie stepped back and motioned Ashleigh to get

going. At the barest urging from Ashleigh, Wonder moved forward. The filly was alert and on her toes, and she trotted onto the track with a bouncy stride. Her head was up and her ears pricked sharply forward. Ashleigh's eyes were forward, too, as she took in the sweep of the empty grandstand, the green infield, the white railings bounding the track. The track was very quiet in the early morning—no cheering crowds, no bustle of activity—just a few trainers, horses, and riders silhouetted in the dawn light and the sounds of pounding hooves and snorted equine breaths.

Ashleigh saw they had a clear opening on the track. She moved Wonder toward the track's center and trotted her up past the grandstand and under the finish wire. Then she let Wonder out into a slow canter.

Wonder sprang into the faster pace, but Ashleigh took a firm grip on the reins, signaling to the filly that they weren't going to do any fast galloping. "Take it easy, girl," Ashleigh said softly. "Let's see what this track is all about."

Wonder flicked back her ears, listening. She didn't fight Ashleigh's gentle pressure on the reins. Like Ashleigh, the filly was looking curiously at her new surroundings as they made the first lap around the track.

Wonder was moving at a smooth, easy canter as they finished lapping the course for the second time. A much larger crowd of horses and trainers were near the entrance now. Ashleigh thought she saw Ken

Maddock, the head trainer at Townsend Acres, but she was too concentrated on the gallop ahead to pay attention. She watched for Charlie's signal, saw it, then dropped her hands and let out the reins slightly. She remained high in the saddle with her knees only partially bent, signaling to Wonder that she wanted a slow pace.

Wonder accelerated into a collected gallop, and Ashleigh moved with the surging strength of the horse beneath her as Wonder's muscles gathered and stretched. She guided the filly in closer to the rail, and they swept around the clubhouse turn. Ashleigh saw the three-quarter pole just ahead. Two strides before the pole, Ashleigh eased slightly on the reins, letting Wonder out another notch. The filly eagerly responded, increasing her speed by the small measure Ashleigh allowed. *So far, so good,* Ashleigh thought. Their pace was exactly what Charlie had asked for.

Then suddenly, as they entered the straight of the backstretch, Wonder thrust her head forward and pulled the reins right through Ashleigh's fingers. Before Ashleigh had time to react, Wonder lunged forward in a breakneck gallop. Ashleigh hauled back on the reins, but Wonder already had the bit in her teeth!

Through Wonder's flying mane, Ashleigh saw a horse galloping down the backstretch in front of them. Wonder had seen it first and was now hot in pursuit.

Sweat broke out on Ashleigh's brow. Wonder

wasn't supposed to galloping at this speed. Charlie was going to be furious. Ashleigh hauled back on the reins again and called desperately to the filly. "Whoa, Wonder. Slow down, girl . . . slow down!"

Wonder wasn't listening. She was intent on catching the horse in front, and nothing was going to stop her. In a panic, Ashleigh remembered her first rides on Wonder that past winter, when she hadn't been able to control the filly. It was happening again! But she *had* to control Wonder now! Ashleigh stood up further in the saddle, lifting her weight away from Wonder's neck. Wonder didn't respond. Her mane whipped back, stinging Ashleigh's cheeks. All Ashleigh could hear was the dull echo of the filly's pounding hooves and Wonder's even, snorted breaths. The reins chafed against her hands, and she felt the strain on her arm and shoulder muscles as she tried to hold back a thousand pounds of headstrong horse.

They rushed past the horse in front like a comet, but still Wonder galloped on at terrifying speed into and around the far turn, then down the stretch toward the wire. She was running as if she were in a race and had to get her head under the wire first. Ashleigh was frantic, but there was nothing she could do now except hold on.

In a blur, she saw Charlie, Jilly, and the other trainers along the rail as they swept past. Charlie was going to kill her! He'd never let her ride Wonder again. And worse, this wild ride might just ruin Wonder for the following day's race!

Only a sixteenth of a mile left to the wire. "Please slow down when we get under that wire," Ashleigh pleaded through gritted teeth. "You've got to!"

Ashleigh hauled on the reins with all of her weakening strength as they raced under the wire. She felt like her arms were going to fall from their sockets. What if Wonder just kept running and running?

Then, amazingly, Wonder began to slow down. Ashleigh nearly fainted with relief. She didn't know if the filly had understood her pleas, or if she intuitively knew that she'd run the course. But suddenly Ashleigh had a perfectly obedient horse beneath her.

Ashleigh gasped. Her whole body was trembling with strain. "That's it, Wonder. Good girl. Let's just keep it nice and slow until we get back to Charlie."

She gradually turned the cantering filly, then slowed Wonder to a trot as they approached the gate. She shuddered at the thought of seeing Charlie's face, hearing his angry words.

There were dozens of people around now—and they all seemed to be staring at her and Wonder. Ashleigh rode through the gate and headed for a spot on the fringe of the crowd. Charlie and Jilly rushed toward her as she drew Wonder to a halt. She patted Wonder's sweaty neck and squeezed her own eyes shut in misery, as if she could block out the memory of the ride.

"You didn't know, girl, did you? It was my fault. I wasn't even thinking about what you'd do if you saw a horse in front of you."

Ashleigh opened her eyes to see Charlie's angry face glaring up at her. Jilly stood nervously by his side.

"I'm sorry," Ashleigh cried breathlessly before Charlie could say a word.

"You weren't paying attention! What the heck were you thinking about?" Charlie barked. "She wouldn't have gotten her head if you'd had her in hand and had your mind on business. You ever want to ride on the track in a race, then you break yourself of that habit right now!"

A hot, embarrassed flush flooded Ashleigh's cheeks. The worst part was that the lecture was well deserved. She felt the prickles of staring eyes. Charlie's reprimand hadn't gone unnoticed by the trainers and riders standing nearby.

Before Charlie had a chance to say more, Ken Maddock walked over to them. He quickly looked Wonder over, then spoke to Charlie.

"Some breeze—a minute nine seconds!" he said. "You're taking kind of a risk though, aren't you, working her that hard now with a race tomorrow?"

"It was my fault," Ashleigh said quickly. "I let her get away going into the backstretch. She was trying to catch the horse in front."

Maddock rubbed his chin and spoke to Charlie. "So

you weren't intending to breeze her that fast? Still, her time confirms what the Townsends are thinking—if she does anything outstanding, she'll do it as a sprinter."

"She'll go the longer distance, too," Charlie said shortly.

Maddock narrowed his eyes, studying Wonder again. "We'll see tomorrow, though I don't think this blowout today's going to help her any." He gave Charlie a nod and walked off.

Ashleigh was mortified. Maddock must think she was an idiot—a totally worthless horsewoman.

"Do you know who you flew past on the backstretch?" Jilly whispered. "Townsend Prince."

"You're kidding," Ashleigh gulped.

"They were only warming him up, not breezing him—but still. . . ."

Charlie turned his full attention to Ashleigh. He motioned for her to dismount. His expression was tight and angry. While Ashleigh held Wonder, he expertly removed her saddle and handed it to Jilly. Then he made a careful inspection of the filly, running his hands over her legs.

"Have I ruined her chances for the race tomorrow?" Ashleigh asked in a small voice.

"Maybe. Maybe not. Just lucky she's in top condition, and she's got guts. Walk her around so I can get a look at her."

Wishing she could just crawl into a hole some-where, Ashleigh led the filly off in a circle around Charlie. As she did, she noticed two men staring at them from the rail—looking especially closely at Wonder. The younger of the two walked over to them.

"Interesting filly," he said to Charlie. "What can you tell me about her?"

Charlie lifted his brows. "Who are you?" he asked curtly.

"Jerry Barns, a handicapper with *The Daily Racing Form*. You the same Charlie Burke I hear used to train for Townsend years back?"

"The same."

"You're training for him again?"

"I'm handling this filly."

"I see she broke her maiden on the first try. But this breeze today is a real eye-opener." Barns paused, waiting. As naive as Ashleigh was about the track, she knew Jerry Barns was hoping to pull some surprise information from Charlie. She knew, too, that he wouldn't have much luck.

Charlie continued watching Wonder as Ashleigh walked her around. He didn't say a word.

Finally Barns spoke. "I see you've got her in a mile allowance tomorrow."

"Yup," Charlie said.

"You think she's ready? Not much of a field, but she looks like a natural sprinter to me. You going to be able to stretch her for another quarter mile, especially after this workout today?"

"She can go the distance." Charlie turned his back on the handicapper and strode over to Wonder and Ashleigh. "I got a horse to take care of," he said. "Let's get her back to the barn and cool her out." He set off, leaving Ashleigh and Jilly to follow.

"Charlie, I'm really sorry—" Ashleigh began.

"What's done is done." When they reached the stabling area, Charlie stopped and turned around. "Sponge her down good, then give her a long walk until she cools out. We'll see what kind of appetite she's got when she gets back to the stall. Jilly, come with me. I want to talk about tomorrow's race."

4

THE NEXT AFTERNOON ASHLEIGH WATCHED FROM THE RAIL AS Jilly and Wonder entered the starting gate for the fifth race. Charlie stood grimly beside her. Ashleigh didn't say a word. She was desperately afraid that she'd ruined Wonder's chances of winning the race, and was fairly sure that Charlie agreed.

Wonder had eaten well the night before. She'd seemed bright and alert that morning when Jilly had worked her very lightly on the track. The racing fans were obviously impressed with her composure during the post parade. Ashleigh glanced to the big board in the infield as the last bets were posted. Wonder had jumped to third betting choice, but that didn't make Ashleigh feel any better. She knew what a strain the race would be on the filly.

In the barn area that morning, everyone had seemed to be speculating on Wonder's breeze, and a steady stream of curious strangers had stopped outside Wonder's stall as Ashleigh groomed her.

Now the horses were in the gate. Wonder had drawn the third post position in the field of eight. Charlie wasn't thrilled with that spot. He was afraid Wonder would be blocked in and had told Jilly to get Wonder right out to the front.

Ashleigh's heart started beating rapidly. The gate sprang open. "And they're off!" the announcer cried.

Wonder broke cleanly, but the horse beside her stumbled coming out of the gate and careened into Wonder, forcing her over. Instead of getting quickly to the lead, Wonder and Jilly were once again caught in the pack, with horses both inside and outside of them and three across the track directly ahead.

Ashleigh could sense the filly's frustration and saw Jilly rise up in the saddle, trying to keep Wonder from climbing over the horses in front of her.

"Hold her," Charlie muttered. "Something's got to give."

Ashleigh wasn't so sure. Two horses had gone to the front and opened up a wide lead on the rest of the field, but the three strung across the track in front of Wonder were having their own speed duel, none of them giving an inch. The horses to either side of Wonder seemed glued in place, though it was obvious Wonder could have outrun them if given the room to move.

The field moved along the backstretch. Then Ashleigh saw the jockey to the outside of Jilly and Wonder go for his whip, trying to edge his mount out and around the pack. Other riders went for their whips. Wonder was suddenly surrounded by flying crops. Ashleigh gasped, knowing what was going to happen. And it did. Wonder seemed to shudder, then she started dropping back. For a moment she seemed to be going in reverse.

"Looks like Ashleigh's Wonder is dropping out of it," the announcer called.

"Oh, Charlie, we've lost it," Ashleigh moaned.

"Not yet. That's it—steady her! Let her drop back, then get her out in the middle."

The field was nearing the end of the backstretch. The same two horses were still in the lead. The rest of the pack was bunched three lengths behind them. Wonder and Jilly were in last place, eleven lengths off the leaders.

But Wonder was running again. Out of sight of the whips, she was back in gear, putting her heart into it. The field was approaching the far turn, jostling for positions for the stretch drive.

Wonder was racing full speed down the center of the track, around the horses that had blocked her before. Jilly was keeping her far away from the whips that had frightened her, but their route meant that Wonder had the longest distance to travel.

The field swept around the turn into the stretch. The two leaders were dueling. They'd increased their lead to six lengths. But Wonder was roaring after them. With each stride, she was narrowing the distance. "Come on, Wonder," Ashleigh breathed, but she knew there was little hope now.

"Break the Bank and Gyro are neck and neck," cried the announcer. "But Ashleigh's Wonder is coming on quickly down the center of the track! The filly had a bad start, but she's rapidly making up ground. Gyro and Break the Bank continue fighting for the lead. Down to the wire they come . . . and it's Break the Bank by a nose! Then Gyro, with Ashleigh's Wonder a half-length back in third."

"Come on," Charlie said shortly. "We've got a horse to see to."

Ashleigh numbly followed him through the bustling crowd along the rail. From the tone of his voice, she was sure he blamed her. They were waiting when Jilly rode Wonder off the track.

The filly looked tired and shaken. Ashleigh's heart plummeted. Jilly was wagging her head. "She gave it everything she had, Charlie. It was rough trip, and she just didn't have enough left."

Ashleigh went to Wonder and eased her hand over the filly's sweat-bathed neck. "I'm so sorry, girl."

Jilly threw her leg over the saddle and dismounted.

"Everything that could go wrong, went wrong, Charlie."

"These things happen. You gave it your best." He turned his attention to Wonder. Jilly quickly removed the light saddle from Wonder's sweaty back. Charlie laid a gentle and experienced hand on the filly's shoulder. "Put your heart in it today, didn't you, little lady? Took a lot out of you. Let's get you cooled out and in your stall."

With Ashleigh leading Wonder, the four of them headed toward the barns. Others on the backside were noticing Wonder's condition. Ashleigh was nagged by guilt. "She would have come out of the race better if I hadn't breezed her so fast yesterday," she said to Charlie.

"Overcoming what she did in this race would have put a strain on her anyway," he answered. "She ran darned well, considering."

"I thought we were finished when I saw those whips," Jilly said. "I could feel her trembling. I didn't think she'd try again, but when I talked to her, she came right back. If I'd been thinking, I would have pulled her back sooner, but I kept hoping for a hole in front."

"No telling how a race will play out, but I think from now on, we'll run her with blinkers."

When they reached the stable yard, Jilly headed off

to the jockeys' rooms. Ashleigh walked the tired filly up and down the yard to cool her out, while Charlie sat on a bench watching Wonder's movements, looking for any signs of lameness. Finally Charlie motioned Ashleigh to bring Wonder to the side of the yard and start washing her down. Ashleigh grabbed a bucket of water. The filly heaved a sigh as the cool liquid splashed over her steaming coat. Ashleigh had never seen Wonder so totally used up. It broke her heart. And no matter what Charlie said, she still felt partially responsible for Wonder's condition.

Ashleigh didn't watch Townsend Prince in the feature race of the day, but as soon as the race was over, she heard the excited talk circulating in the stables. The Prince had won, leading the field from gate to wire and winning by eight lengths.

From Wonder's stall, Ashleigh saw the Townsends arrive with smiles of victory. They were surrounded by reporters. Townsend Prince was receiving heavy attention from the press. Brad had decked himself out for the occasion, wearing a tailored white suit that set off his dark tan. But Brad and his father weren't alone. Two other beautifully dressed people were included in their group—an older man and an absolutely gorgeous girl who looked like his daughter. She was blond and expensively dressed, and she was flirting blatantly with Brad. Brad was eating it up, flashing smiles, leaning over to speak quietly in her diamond-studded ears.

Ashleigh felt a sharp stab of anger. What was Brad doing, flirting around, when her sister was sitting at home? Ashleigh remembered that Caro had said Mr. Townsend was bringing business associates to the race. The girl and her father could be prospective clients, on the verge of buying a very expensive horse from the Townsends. Maybe Brad was being ridiculously nice to the daughter to smooth the way. But Ashleigh had never seen Brad treat her sister so sweetly!

Soon the Townsend party left the stable area, and Ashleigh put the incident out of her mind. She had enough to do looking after her exhausted filly.

By the next morning Wonder seemed more rested and alert, and she was finally eating. Ashleigh and Charlie checked her over carefully and took her out of her stall for a walk around the stable yard. As they did, someone came up and tapped Charlie's shoulder. Ashleigh recognized Jerry Barns, the handicapper from *The Daily Racing Form.*

"Thought you'd like to see this," he said to Charlie. Barns handed Charlie a paper and pointed to the bottom of the folded page before walking away.

Charlie skimmed the article and handed it to Ashleigh. "Might cheer you up a bit," he said. "You've been walking around with a long face since you blew that breeze."

Ashleigh looked down and read the small, two-paragraph article Charlie was pointing to.

"Ashleigh's Wonder (Townsend Pride—Townsend Holly by Renegade), as her breeding suggests, looks like a filly to watch. Although she's been downplayed by the Townsend establishment, she's being trained by Charlie Burke, Eclipse Award trainer—"

Ashleigh stared at Charlie. "I didn't know you won an Eclipse Award!"

Charlie shrugged. "Just keep reading."

Ashleigh did.

"We all thought he was retired, and it's a pleasure to see him back. This Friday Ashleigh's Wonder clocked a six-furlong breeze at Pimlico in 1:09 —impressive, and that despite her rider doing everything but choke the filly to hold her back. Yesterday she ran in a mile allowance race at Pimlico. She finished third, but against incredible adversity. Bumped out of the gate, blocked behind the other runners—obviously whip shy. She fell back and was running last by eleven lengths coming into the far turn. At the finish this filly, ridden outstandingly by Jilly Gordon, was up in third, a half-length off the leaders and gaining with every stride. Definitely a filly to watch. A real game effort."

The article was at the bottom of a page, where few people would notice it, but Ashleigh felt like she'd just read a front-page headline.

"Charlie, this is fantastic!"

"It's the facts," Charlie said.

5

BRIGHTLY COLORED LEAVES CRUNCHED UNDER ASHLEIGH'S FEET as she ran down the drive of Townsend Acres on an early October morning. The bus was rounding the curve at the top of the hill. She would just make it. She was later than usual. With Wonder in serious training, the filly's morning workouts on the track were critical, and Charlie was a slave driver, working both the filly and Ashleigh at an unrelenting pace. He'd talked Townsend into entering Wonder in one more race that fall—a mile-and-a-sixteenth, Grade 2 stakes race at Keeneland in Lexington. And this time he intended to win. So did Ashleigh, of course, but Charlie seemed to have forgotten that Ashleigh now had school every weekday as well.

As the bus drew to a stop, Ashleigh sprinted the last strides and breathlessly climbed on.

"Running late today," the driver said with a grin.

"Yeah," Ashleigh gasped as she headed down the aisle and slid into her usual seat beside Linda.

"Where's Caroline?" Linda asked.

"She didn't feel good this morning and decided to stay home." Ashleigh slid her backpack off her shoulder and balanced it on her jean-clad lap.

"She must be feeling pretty rotten. She hardly ever misses school."

"I know, but she's been acting weird the last few days. She must have some kind of a bug—I sure hope it's not contagious. I can't afford to miss any workouts, especially with the race this weekend. How about riding with me this afternoon?" Ashleigh added. "Charlie wants me to work Wonder over the trails."

"Sure, I'd love to."

"Great! It's absolutely nuts at the farm," Ashleigh said. "All everyone talks about is the Breeder's Cup next month. Brad's been walking around with this big grin on his face all the time."

"What do you expect? Townsend Prince looks like a sure thing to win the Juvenile division, especially after he just won the Champagne at Belmont."

The bus pulled up in front of the school complex. Ashleigh and Linda joined the line of kids filing off the bus and headed for their lockers. For the third year in a row they'd lucked out and had the same homeroom. Ashleigh hoped they'd have the same luck when they went into high school the following year.

"Hi, guys!" Corey Jacobs turned from her locker as the girls passed.

Both Ashleigh and Linda stopped in their tracks and stared at Corey. "What did you do to your hair?" Linda asked.

"You like it?" Corey smoothed her hand over what was left of her pale hair. The day before it had been shoulder length. Now it was shaped to her head in a pixie cut. Corey was grinning and obviously knew it looked good.

"Yeah," Ashleigh said, "I do. You just look so different. You didn't say anything about getting it cut."

"I wanted to surprise everyone."

"What did Bobby say?" Linda asked of Corey's longtime boyfriend and the star of the Henry Clay Middle School football team.

Corey's eyes twinkled. "He freaked at first, but when Jason Fry told me it looked great, Bobby changed his mind. You know Bobby's jealous because he thinks Jason wants to ask me out."

Linda narrowed her eyes and studied Ashleigh. "You know, Ash, your hair might look good that short."

"No way!" Ashleigh cried. "It's bad enough that my sister's always trying to do make-overs on me. I like my hair just fine."

Suddenly Corey looked sly. "Your sister's still going out with Brad Townsend, isn't she?"

"Yes," Ashleigh answered. "Why?"

"Oh, Jennifer was asking me. She said something about seeing him at the country club with someone else." Corey looked like she was about to say more, but Linda broke in.

"Hey, we better get going or we'll be late to homeroom."

"See ya at lunch!" Corey called, heading off in the opposite direction.

"What was that all about?" Linda asked as the girls wove their way up the hall.

Ashleigh shrugged. Jennifer was definitely the prettiest girl in their class, looked at least two years older, and knew exactly how popular she was with the boys. "If I know Jennifer, she's probably hoping she'll get a chance to go out with him. But please, let's talk about something besides Brad Townsend," Ashleigh groaned.

Linda laughed. "Sorry."

Ashleigh met Linda at her locker after their last class. "Matthews clobbered us with homework tonight. I'll probably be up till eleven getting it done. Five pages of translation!"

"Me, too," Linda sighed. "And I hate French worse than anything!"

"Why don't you stay for supper, and we'll work on

it together? My mother or Caroline can give you a ride home."

"Oh, right, I keep forgetting Caroline's got her license now."

"She drives like she's on a racetrack all the time."

"Probably because she's used to racing around in Brad's Ferrari," Linda said. "Oops. I'm not supposed to mention that name."

When the bus dropped them at Townsend Acres, they jogged up the drive under the turning leaves, then hurried into Ashleigh's house and up to her bedroom to change into riding clothes.

Caroline was in bed with the curtains drawn across the windows when the two girls entered the room. Ashleigh walked over and looked down at her sister. "You still feel crummy?" she asked quietly, noticing Caroline's red-rimmed eyes.

Caroline grunted and pulled the covers farther over her face.

"Maybe Mom should call the doctor."

"No," Caroline croaked.

"Okay. We're just going to change. We'll be out of here in a second."

And they were. But as they walked up the drive past the breeding barns, Ashleigh's mother came out of one of the barns.

"How's Caroline?" Mrs. Griffen asked.

"Not very good," Ashleigh answered.

Her mother frowned. "I think it's just a cold, but I'll go in and see if I can get her anything."

The girls continued on to the stables and found Charlie already waiting with Wonder and Belle, both saddled and ready to go. The stables were quiet in the afternoon, and many of the grooms were sitting on benches, cleaning and polishing tack, enjoying the fall weather.

Charlie nodded to the girls. "So you're riding today, too," he said to Linda. "Better go down to the paddock and get Dominator."

Linda was soon back with the big bay horse, who was prancing like a colt, thrilled to be going out for a ride. Linda quickly tacked him up, and within minutes they had all swung up into their saddles and were heading out along the trails between the paddocks.

Even though she'd had a brisk workout that morning, Wonder was in high spirits. She pranced along beside Dominator and Linda, shaking her head and sending her silky mane dancing.

Ashleigh patted the filly's arched neck and took a deep breath of the crisp, clear air. There hadn't been a frost yet, and the grass was still a brilliant green under the blue skies. "What do you want to do today, Charlie?" she asked the old trainer, who was riding beside her.

"A long canter—four or five miles. I want to work on her stamina. If we're going to point her to the Triple Crown, then she's got to go a mile and a half at a gallop without stressing herself. Going across country, up and down hills, is the best way to build up her lungs and muscles."

Ashleigh stared at the trainer. This was the first time he'd actually come out and said anything about the Triple Crown. "You mean it, Charlie?" she asked excitedly. "You're heading her for the Triple Crown?"

"Thought that was what you wanted."

"Yes, but—"

"Too soon to tell yet anyway. A lot can happen between now and the first weekend in May. Okay, they're warmed up enough. Let's canter 'em." Charlie immediately heeled Belle forward.

Ashleigh glanced quickly at Linda. Linda beamed a grin and gave Ashleigh a thumbs-up sign. The two of them put Wonder and Dominator into a canter, following Charlie.

The trio pounded smoothly over the lush grass, up to the crest of the hill that overlooked the huge expanse of Townsend Acres. From the crest, they headed down into tree-shaded dips and over the rolling countryside between the white-fenced paddocks. They left the barns and stables far behind and rode to the very limits of the farm before curving back toward the training area.

Ashleigh sat back in the gently rocking gait of Wonder's canter. She could tell from Wonder's sharply pricked ears that the filly was enjoying the outing as much as her rider. Even Charlie was content to ride along in silence without his usual barked comments.

It seemed no time at all until Charlie pulled Belle back to a trot and motioned to the girls to do the same. "Five miles and then some," he said. He drew up parallel to Ashleigh and carefully looked Wonder over. "She's hardly worked up a sweat. Good. Think we'll give her another work like this tomorrow. That should put her in good shape for the weekend."

They trotted the horses the remaining mile back to the stables. Charlie studied Wonder critically, watching the filly's movements.

"She feels good, Charlie," Ashleigh told him. Then her eye was caught by two riders walking their mounts under the trees a dozen yards away. They were moving away along a side trail, but even from the back Ashleigh recognized Brad. The girl on the horse next to him wasn't Caroline. The girl turned her head, and Ashleigh knew she'd seen her before—in the stables at Pimlico.

Linda saw them, too. She swung to Ashleigh, but Ashleigh motioned her to be quiet. She didn't want to say anything in front of Charlie.

They rode back to the stable yard in silence, but Ashleigh's head was spinning. What should she do? Should she tell Caroline? How could Brad do this? Taking another girl riding right on the farm!

Ashleigh barely heard Charlie's last instructions as they stopped in front of the stable and dismounted, but she knew exactly what to do anyway—untack the filly, throw a light sheet over her, walk her up and down the yard until she was completely cool, then take her to her stall and groom and feed her. She nodded mutely as Charlie untacked Belle and led the mare off.

Only when Charlie was gone did Ashleigh turn to Linda. "I've seen that girl before, at Pimlico! She and a man who looked like her father were with the Townsends."

"I don't believe it!" Linda gasped. "What's her name?"

"I don't know. I saw them from across the barn—but I can tell you one thing: she looked rich."

"Are you going to tell Caroline?"

Ashleigh started leading Wonder off, and Linda walked Dominator beside her. "I don't know," Ashleigh said. "Caroline will freak. And she's already sick. Maybe Brad and that girl are just friends."

Linda gave Ashleigh a look.

"Yeah, I know. They didn't look like just friends."

They finished putting the horses away and went back to Ashleigh's for dinner. Ashleigh still hadn't decided what to do. Mrs. Griffen smiled at the girls as they came into the kitchen. "Can you set the table, Ashleigh?" she asked.

"How's Caro?" Ashleigh said as she collected plates from the cupboard and silverware from the drawer. Linda took the silverware from Ashleigh's hand and started setting places.

"Sleeping," Mrs. Griffen answered. "I just checked on her a few minutes ago. I'll bring her up some soup, so don't set a place for her."

Rory came bursting into the kitchen. "Guess what, Ash?" he cried. "Dad said I could help April bring in the weanlings! We just finished."

"So how'd you do?" Ashleigh asked. Rory was in good hands with April, one of the longtime breeding grooms. The red-haired young woman had befriended Ashleigh when they'd first moved to the farm, and had helped a lot during Wonder's rough early months of life.

"Great," Rory said. "There's one foal I really like. Remember, I showed him to you in the spring. Kelsy's foal."

"That little bay with the white blaze?"

"Yeah, that one. Mr. Townsend and Brad don't pay much attention to him, but I think he's going to be one of the best."

"Are you trying to find another Wonder?" Linda smiled.

For a second Rory frowned, not sure what to make of Linda's teasing tone. "Why not? He *could* be."

"I'm not saying he couldn't," Linda added quickly. "Picking unexpected winners must run in the family."

Rory grinned. "You and Ashleigh can help me train him."

"Don't you think you're jumping the gun a little?" Mrs. Griffen said from the stove. "The foal's not even six months old. It'll be a while before he goes into training, and Mr. Maddock may like him enough to train him himself."

Ashleigh and Rory exchanged a wink. Their parents had used the same words of caution when Ashleigh had decided she wanted to train Wonder. "Linda and I will come down to the barn with you after supper to look at him. I wanted to visit Holly anyway." Ashleigh would always feel a strong bond with Wonder's dam, Holly. Wonder had been the old mare's last foal. Holly had been retired for a well-deserved rest, but whenever Ashleigh could find the time, she stopped by Holly's stall for a chat with her old friend.

"Rory, run down and tell your father supper's ready," Mrs. Griffen said. "And remember, it's your night to do dishes."

"Oh, yuck!"

"And make sure you wash your hands when you get back."

Rory dashed off, and a few minutes later Mr. Griffen strode into the kitchen. "I thought you were going

53

to remind me to come up and cook tonight," he said to his wife.

"You were too busy with Three-Foot. You can do the honors tomorrow. How's the mare?"

"So far so good, though I'm afraid she may still lose her foal. Townsend's concerned—you know what kind of hopes he has for this foal. It would be a full sibling to Townsend Prince." He turned to Ashleigh and Linda. "How was the ride this afternoon? Wonder all set for the race this weekend?"

"Charlie's happy," Ashleigh said.

"She had some tough breaks last race. She'll do fine."

But Ashleigh knew her father's idea of Wonder's doing fine and hers were different. He shared the feeling of the rest of the staff in the stables that, at a mile and a sixteenth, with the competition she was up against, Wonder would be doing well if she finished third.

After dinner and a quick visit to the breeding barns with Rory, Ashleigh and Linda went to the den to work on their French assignment. "I still don't know whether to tell Caro or not," Ashleigh said, frowning.

"She's already sick. I don't think you should." Linda paused in her writing and ran the end of her pen through her curls.

"Yeah. Besides, I'm *afraid* to tell her."

"I would be, too," Linda said. "She's so crazy about Brad. This whole thing is really a mess."

The two of them concentrated on their homework until it was finished, then Ashleigh pulled a copy of *The Daily Racing Form* from the back of her notebook. The girls spent ten minutes studying the articles on various horses and their recorded breezing times.

At nine, Mrs. Griffen gave Linda a ride home, and Ashleigh went quietly upstairs, still debating what to do about Brad. She didn't want to keep something so important from Caroline—it made her feel like a traitor—but she didn't have the courage to tell Caroline, either.

She silently eased open their bedroom door, intending to get her pajamas and change in the bathroom. But as she slipped across the darkened room, she heard muffled sobs coming from Caroline's bed. She flicked on the soft light on the night table she and Caro shared and leaned over Caro's bed. "Caro, what's wrong?" she asked worriedly. "Do you feel that bad?"

Caro continued sobbing.

Ashleigh laid a hand on her sister's shoulder. "Should I get Mom?"

"No," Caroline said hoarsely.

"But why are you crying?"

Caroline gasped back another sob and just shook her blond head. Ashleigh had never seen her sister's hair looking like such a mess.

55

"There must be something wrong. What is it?" Ashleigh pleaded.

Ashleigh had to lean closer to hear her sister's ragged response.

"It's Brad . . ."

Ashleigh froze and waited. Did Caroline already know?

In a moment Caroline turned to face Ashleigh, then covered her face with her hands. "He . . . he broke up with me!" Caroline erupted in fresh sobs.

"Oh, no," Ashleigh whispered. "When?"

"Two days ago."

"Oh, Caro, why didn't you say anything?"

"I couldn't . . . I kept hoping he didn't mean it. Ash, he didn't even tell me to my face! He called Tuesday night like he always does . . . but . . . but he just said he wouldn't be seeing me anymore . . . that it wasn't working. I tried to ask him why, but he said he couldn't talk. He was at the club. He sounded so cold . . . and then he said he had to go, and hung up."

Ashleigh thought about what she'd seen that afternoon and gritted her teeth in anger. She sure couldn't tell Caroline about it now!

"There's more, Ashleigh," Caro said brokenly. "I couldn't believe what Brad said on the phone. I was sure he would change his mind." Caro closed her eyes in pain. "I . . . I went up to the stables yesterday afternoon to talk to him. He was there talking to some of the grooms. I asked him if I could talk to him privately . . . and right in front of the grooms, he said, 'There's nothing to talk about. I meant what I said on the phone the other night. We're finished, so let's just forget it.' Then he turned his back on me and started talking to the grooms like nothing was wrong. I wanted to *die.* They were all staring at me. Oh, Ash, what am I going to do?"

Ashleigh reached out and held her trembling sister. It was worse than she'd expected. How could Brad act like that? They'd been going together for nine months. If he was going to break up with her, at least he could be decent about it—and not embarrass her in front of everyone. No wonder Caroline hadn't been able to go to school. "Didn't he give you any warning?" Ashleigh asked softly.

Caroline shook her head. "He had to break a date with me last weekend because he was doing something with his father . . . but I didn't even guess."

Ashleigh looked at her sister's swollen, red-rimmed eyes and knew that she had to do something to help. She'd never understood why Caro and so many other girls were nutty about Brad. To Ashleigh he'd always seemed like an arrogant, conceited snob not worth bothering about. She wasn't going to let him hurt her sister like this.

"How am I going to face everyone at school?" Caro

sobbed. "I know how many girls have been hoping we'd break up, so they could go out with him. . . ."

"You've got to fight back, Caro! Don't let Brad know how hurt you are. Act like you're glad that you split up—that you were getting bored with him anyway."

"But I'm *not* glad!"

"You'd rather everyone felt sorry for you?" Ashleigh shot back.

"No . . ."

"Then go to school tomorrow and don't let anyone see how upset you are."

"I can't. As soon as I tell anyone, I know I'll start to cry."

"Don't tell anyone, then. And don't hang around here all weekend, either. Come to Keeneland with me to watch Wonder race."

"But Brad might be there!" Caroline exclaimed.

"I don't think so. Townsend Prince has been shipped to Belmont to get ready for the Breeder's Cup. Townsend Acres doesn't have any big horses running at Keeneland this weekend. Why would Brad bother going?"

"I suppose you're right," Caroline said weakly.

"Come with me. It'll be better than sitting around here."

"All right . . . Ash . . . I know you never liked me going out with Brad. I feel like a real jerk now."

"You're not a jerk—he is!"

6

ASHLEIGH LOOKED FOR BRAD THE NEXT MORNING DURING THE workouts, but she didn't see him. With Townsend Prince in New York, Brad didn't have to come to the oval to exercise him. Ashleigh felt cheated. She'd lain awake the night before, thinking about what she'd say to Brad about the way he'd treated Caroline.

But as Charlie motioned her and Wonder out onto the oval, she had to put Caroline's problems out of her mind. Charlie was watching them critically, and so were the other trainers and the riders waiting to go out onto the track. A few minutes before, one of the younger grooms, Terry Bush, had filled Ashleigh in on the latest stable talk.

"Wonder had a bum rap in her last race, but they still don't think she can win at a mile and a sixteenth."

"Who's 'they'?" Ashleigh had asked coldly.

"Most everyone, actually. A lot of us want to see

you and Charlie do it. We like the filly, but there are a lot of good two-year-old fillies out there. She's going to be racing against one of them Saturday—Charad. The talk is that Charad's trainer expects her to walk all over the field."

"Well, we'll prove them wrong," Ashleigh said.

Wonder performed like a dream that morning, clocking one of her best breezes yet. Ashleigh patted her proudly as they pranced off the oval. Even Charlie's old eyes were twinkling.

"I don't know if I want to go, Ashleigh," Caroline said uncertainly as the two girls climbed into the family station wagon on Saturday morning.

"You have to go now, Caro. How else am I going to get there if you don't drive me?"

"I should have told you last night so you could have gone over with Jilly and Charlie."

"Too late now," Ashleigh snapped more sharply than she'd intended. But she wasn't going to miss Wonder's race! And it would do Caroline good to get away from the farm.

"But what if Brad's there?" Caroline moaned as she started the car.

"He won't be."

"I still feel so awful."

"Come on, Caro," Ashleigh soothed. "It's only been

a couple of days, and you won't feel any better hanging around here."

Sighing heavily, Caroline backed up the car and headed down the drive. Ashleigh tried to keep up a light chatter as they followed the familiar roads to Lexington, past acres of white-fenced paddocks fringed by brightly colored trees. But Caroline was off in a daze and didn't seem to hear a word Ashleigh said. A half hour later Caroline pulled off the road toward the backside of the beautiful Keeneland track. She found a spot near the barn where the Townsend Acres horses were usually stabled, parked, and turned off the engine.

"You'll feel better when you get out with other people," Ashleigh said, trying her best to cheer Caroline up. Caroline just shrugged.

They found Charlie outside Wonder's stall. He nodded a greeting to the girls. Ashleigh had told him the night before that Caroline was giving her a ride. If he'd been surprised, he hadn't said anything. But then he'd probably already heard the stable gossip about Brad and Caro breaking up.

Wonder stuck her head over the stall door, and Ashleigh hurried over to the filly and fed her the bits of carrot she'd stashed in her jacket pocket. "You're looking full of it, girl," Ashleigh grinned. "How'd she work this morning, Charlie?"

Charlie shifted his hat back on his head. "Only did

a light work to limber her up, but she seemed nice and smooth. Jilly said she felt good."

Ashleigh dropped a kiss on Wonder's soft muzzle. "You're going to show them today, aren't you?"

"Let's hope," Charlie said.

Ashleigh glanced over at her sister. Caroline was anxiously looking up and down the line of stalls at the many grooms, trainers, and other visitors bustling around. Ashleigh knew who she was looking for. Ashleigh turned to Charlie and whispered, "Who's here from Townsend Acres?"

Charlie seemed to understand the reason for her question. "Only Maddock and the grooms so far."

Ashleigh nodded with relief. It wasn't likely Brad would come to the track for the horses that were running. She gave Wonder a quick hug. "I'll be back to groom you before the race. Caro, let's go see if we can find Linda."

Caro gave a disinterested shrug.

"Be back here at one," Charlie called as the girls headed off.

Ashleigh led Caroline through the stabling area, toward the barn where Linda and her father kept their horses. Linda was walking a coal black colt outside the barn. She saw Ashleigh and Caroline and waved. "Hi, guys. I was wondering when you'd get here. Just let me put him in his stall."

Ashleigh had told Linda all about Caro and Brad but

had sworn her to silence. Linda quickly stabled the horse and hurried over. "I'm glad you came, Caro," she said. "You can help us cheer Wonder on. How's she look?" she added to Ashleigh.

"Good."

Caroline still seemed in a daze. Linda gave Ashleigh a questioning look. Ashleigh just lifted her shoulders.

"Let's check out some of the other horses," Linda suggested, "and we can get some lunch before the races start."

But Linda's enthusiasm was wasted on Caroline. Caroline followed silently behind Ashleigh and Linda as they looked over the occupants of dozens of stalls. Caroline didn't even pretend to be interested in the horses, but Ashleigh saw how carefully her sister inspected the crowd of people.

Ashleigh finally gave up trying to distract her sister and talked horses with Linda. "What have you heard about Charad?" she asked.

Linda frowned. "That she's good. She worked a mile in 1:35 the other day. Everyone's talking about it. Her stall's up here. Come and take a look."

Ashleigh wasn't sure she wanted to take too close a look at Wonder's competition, and when she saw Charad, she felt her stomach sink. The gray filly was big, a couple of inches taller than Wonder, and she looked ready to go. She had her head over the stall door and was alertly watching everything going on in the yard.

Ashleigh grunted. "She looks good, doesn't she?"

"Wonder can beat her," Linda said encouragingly.

Ashleigh turned away from Charad's stall. For the first time that day, she felt the beginnings of pre-race jitters. She didn't want to start worrying about the race yet, or Wonder would pick up on her nervousness when Ashleigh groomed her. "Let's go get something to eat. I'm starved," she said.

By the time Ashleigh had finished grooming Wonder two hours later, she was feeling as if she'd brought a zombie with her to the track. Caroline had barely said two words, not even in complaint. Ashleigh wondered if it had been such a good idea coaxing her sister to come. Caroline's misery was distracting her, and it was Wonder who needed Ashleigh now.

In the pre-race bustle, Ashleigh tried to push Caroline's problems from her mind. Wonder was growing excited. The filly knew what was coming up, and Ashleigh had to soothe her—keep the horse as calm as possible. She was relieved when Charlie finally gave Jilly a leg into the saddle, and the horses started their parade out to the track.

"Let's go," Charlie said, shuffling off in the direction of the grandstand. Ashleigh lightly gripped Caroline's arm and led her along. Half of her mind was on the race ahead—the other half was on her brooding sister.

There had still been no sign of any of the Townsends before the race, so if Wonder won, it would be up to Charlie to go to the winner's circle. The three of them squeezed in near the rail at the front of the grandstand seats where they'd have a clear view of the track. Ashleigh lifted her glasses and watched as the field approached the starting gate. Charad definitely did look good, and the betting crowd had her as an even-money favorite. But they'd been lucky with Wonder's post position this time. She was number seven into the gate. The filly went in smoothly.

Ashleigh turned to Caroline. "Want to look through the glasses?"

Caroline shook her head. "No, I can see all right." For the first time there was a slight lift to Caro's voice, Ashleigh noticed. Maybe her sister was finally snapping out of it, but Ashleigh didn't have time to dwell on it. The horses were in the gate. The gate doors flew open.

"They're off!" the announcer shouted.

Wonder broke cleanly and went right to the lead. Ashleigh felt a wave of relief. This time there wouldn't be horses blocking her progress.

"That's the way," Charlie mumbled as Jilly moved Wonder over close to the rail, a half-length in front of the rest of the field. Ashleigh could see that Wonder wanted to put out more, but Jilly had her firmly in check, saving the filly's stamina for the stretch run.

Behind Wonder on the outside, Charad was rapidly gaining, and the two fillies were leaving the rest of the field behind. Wonder held on to the half-length lead, but the pace was blazing. They'd run the first half mile in close to track-record time. Ashleigh held her breath as the horses pounded down the backstretch. At this rate, Wonder would use up everything before she even got into the final stretch.

Suddenly Ashleigh heard Caro's voice beside her. "Come on, Wonder," Caroline said softly. "Win this one for the Griffens."

Ashleigh could barely believe what she heard. Caroline was snapping out of her daze.

On her other side, Ashleigh heard Charlie mumble, "Hold her till the turn. Don't let that filly pressure you!"

"Will Wonder have anything left?" Ashleigh asked Charlie anxiously.

"She should. We'll see."

The crowd in the grandstand was going wild. Wonder and Charad came off the turn with Wonder barely a half-length in the lead. Charad's jockey went for his whip.

"Now!" Charlie barked. "Let her out!"

Ashleigh saw Jilly do just that. She loosened the tension on Wonder's reins, leaned down tight over Wonder's withers, and kneaded her hands along the filly's neck.

Wonder shot forward.

"She still has something!" Ashleigh cried.

Charlie wrenched his hat from his head and clenched it in his hand. "So does the other filly."

Charad, under the prodding of the whip, shot forward, too. But Wonder wasn't about to be caught. She was flying, running with all her heart—doing what she liked doing best.

"Go, Wonder!" Caroline screamed.

Ashleigh lowered her binoculars and clenched them with both hands. "That's the way, girl. That's the way! You can do it!"

Wonder and Jilly swept past them down the stretch. Charad was right off Wonder's flank, but Charad was struggling. Wonder gained another length before she swept under the wire, beating one of the best two-year-old fillies on the East Coast—decisively!

"All right!" Ashleigh cried. She spun around and grabbed Caroline and hugged her. Caroline was laughing, finally forgetting her misery. Ashleigh turned and hugged Charlie, too. "She did it, Charlie!"

"Yup," the old man said with gruff embarrassment at the physical display. He quickly ducked his head and slapped his hat back in place, hiding his smile of victory. "We'd better get down to the winner's circle."

They pushed through the crowd. Caroline was smiling and looking smug. She leaned closer and spoke in

Ashleigh's ear. "I'm so glad she won and proved Brad was wrong!"

"You're not the only one," Ashleigh winked back.

As they struggled through the crowd around the winner's circle, Jilly was dismounting. Her face was flushed with happiness. She reached up and patted Wonder's neck, and the filly tossed her head in acknowledgment.

Ashleigh rushed into the winner's circle with Charlie. Caroline hurried along behind as Ashleigh went to Wonder's side. "What a race, Jilly," Ashleigh cried. "Perfect. It couldn't have been better!"

"Thanks," Jilly beamed. "She was on—all the way."

Wonder twisted her head and butted Ashleigh's shoulder. "I haven't forgotten you," Ashleigh said with a laugh, rubbing the filly's head. "You were great, girl!"

Wonder snorted proudly. Ashleigh took the reins as Jilly removed the light racing saddle so that she could weigh out.

Ashleigh saw a reporter pushing in close to Charlie. "Surprised about the outcome?" the reporter asked. It was Jerry Barns of *The Daily Racing Form.*

"Nope," Charlie said. "She's a good filly, but I think you knew that."

"You have any thoughts about what happened to Charad?"

"She got outrun."

Barns laughed. Then the crowd behind him and Charlie split. Ashleigh heard someone else call, "Here's one of the owners."

Ashleigh saw Brad come into the winner's circle, and his new girlfriend was on his arm, smiling up at him. Ashleigh swung around in time to see the absolute shock on Caroline's face—then Caroline's face turned ashen. Before Ashleigh could say a word, Caroline spun on her heel and forced her way out of the circle.

"Caroline, wait!" Ashleigh cried. But Caroline kept going, running now. Ashleigh had to catch her—Caroline was upset enough to do something stupid.

Charlie and Jilly had both seen Caroline's reaction. Brad had seen Caroline, too, but he didn't seem even slightly upset. Ashleigh handed Wonder's reins to the trainer. "Can you hold her, Charlie? I've got to go after Caro."

Charlie nodded, and Ashleigh pushed through the crowd in pursuit. Instinct told her that Caroline would head for the car, and Ashleigh knew Caroline was in no state to drive. She was a wild driver anyway. She'd take her anger out on the road.

Ashleigh's heart was pounding as she raced out of the grandstand and through the stabling area, dodging horses and grooms. She'd lost sight of Caro, but she took the fastest route to the parking area. She came out from behind the last barn and saw Caro already at the door of the station wagon, keys in hand.

Panting, Ashleigh tried to get to the car, but Caroline had the engine started and was backing up.

"No, Caro!" Ashleigh shouted. "Wait!"

She was too late. With squealing tires, Caroline accelerated and zoomed out of the lot.

7

ASHLEIGH'S PARENTS WERE WAITING IN THE KITCHEN WHEN Ashleigh burst into the house late that afternoon. "I should never have taken her to the race," Ashleigh cried. "I should have guessed Brad might turn up."

Her mother got up quickly from the table and hugged Ashleigh. "It's not your fault."

"She wouldn't have had an accident if she had stayed home!" Ashleigh said.

"You can't look at it that way," her father said firmly. "Let's just be thankful she came out of it with only a broken arm and some abrasions. It could have been much worse."

Ashleigh slid down into a kitchen chair. "Where is she? Up in the bedroom?"

Her mother nodded. "She's sleeping. The doctor gave her a mild sedative."

"And Rory?"

"He was visiting his friend Brian," Mrs. Griffen said. "I called and asked if he could spend the night."

"Is the car wrecked?"

"The front fender's completely smashed," Mr. Griffen answered, "and the passenger door's badly scraped, but it's fixable."

"How did it happen?" Ashleigh asked.

"Caroline didn't remember very clearly afterward," Mr. Griffen said. "She said something about the tires skidding. It looks like she lost control on a corner and went off the road into a tree. Thank heavens she didn't hit it head-on."

Ashleigh's mother sighed. "I just wish I'd known she and Brad had broken up. I could have talked to her. Why didn't you tell me?"

"Caro didn't want to tell anyone yet. She was too hurt. She couldn't really talk about it."

Mrs. Griffen frowned. "Brad was her first serious boyfriend, which makes it even worse."

Ashleigh pushed back her chair. "I'll go up and see her."

"Just don't wake her," her mother said quickly. "Sleep's the best thing for her right now. The doctor wants her to rest."

Ashleigh nodded and quickly left the room. She felt shaken when she tiptoed across the bedroom and looked down at her sister. Caro's left arm was in a cast. Her face was as white as the pillow beneath her head—except where darkening bruises discolored her skin. *Oh, Caro,* Ashleigh moaned silently. *How could you let Brad Townsend get to you like that?*

Ashleigh gently adjusted the covers on her sister's bed, then turned and went quietly from the room. Wonder would be arriving back from the track in the van soon, and Ashleigh would need to be in the stable to get her settled. Her joy in Wonder's win was overshadowed by Caro's accident. As she walked up the drive, she shuddered, remembering the stricken expression on Caro's face when she'd seen Brad and his new girlfriend.

The last few hours seemed like a nightmare. Ashleigh hadn't known what to do when Caroline had driven off. In panic, she'd rushed back to tell Jilly and Charlie what had happened, but Jilly couldn't leave the track—she was riding in another race. Charlie no longer had his driver's license. Ashleigh had almost called her parents, then decided that would only frighten them—besides, Caroline would be furious. All Ashleigh could do as she tended to Wonder after the race was to pray Caroline got home safely. But two hours later, her parents had called from the emergency room.

Terry Bush came up to Ashleigh as she approached the barn. The news had spread quickly around the stable yard. The Griffens had had to borrow one of the stable's cars to go to the hospital. "I heard about your sister's accident," he said sadly. "She'll be okay?"

"Eventually."

"Jilly thought it had something to do with Brad and his new girl," Terry said. "He was here with her before they left for Keeneland."

"Yeah. Caroline was pretty upset. Is he back yet?"

"Been and gone. Tell your sister all the guys here were asking for her."

"I will."

"That filly of yours was something today," Terry said in parting. "You've opened a few eyes."

Ashleigh smiled weakly. "I'm proud of her."

Charlie and Jilly were inside the stable talking to some of the other grooms as Ashleigh stepped through the door. She noticed the somber glances sent her way.

"What's the news?" Charlie said quickly. "She going to be all right?"

Ashleigh told them of Caro's injuries and the details of the accident. Charlie frowned and shook his head. Jilly was more vocal. "Brad breezed through here a half hour ago. You know, he didn't say a word about the accident!"

"He probably didn't know yet," Ashleigh said, giving Brad the benefit of the doubt.

"With all the talk around here, he must have found out right after he got here. He had plenty to say about

74

Wonder's race, though," Jilly growled. "All of a sudden the Townsends are interested in her."

"I could have told you that would happen," Charlie said.

"Did you talk to Brad?" Ashleigh asked Charlie.

"Never came near me."

"I can guess why," Ashleigh seethed. "You'd tell him exactly what you thought. I suppose now they'll want to start interfering in her training."

"Not if I have anything to say about it," Charlie said flatly. "I hear the van. Let's get the filly unloaded. Give her a hot bran mash tonight as a reward."

Caroline slept until early afternoon on Sunday. The long sleep worried Ashleigh. "Shouldn't you call the doctor, Mom?" she asked nervously. "Something must be wrong."

"The doctor said to expect this. They did a full set of X-rays at the hospital, and there's no sign of head injuries except the bruising. She needs the rest to heal —emotionally and physically."

Ashleigh was too restless to stay in the house and went up to the stables to talk to Jilly and Charlie. Charlie handed her the sports section from the Sunday *Lexington Herald.* "Got some publicity yesterday, anyway."

The article he pointed to was a post-race interview with Charlie and Brad. There was a review of the race, with glowing comments about Wonder's performance. Then the reporter went on:

"When asked about plans for the filly's three-year-old season, Charlie Burke, her trainer, said he's optimistic, if the filly continues improving as she's done over the fall. Brad Townsend, however, son of the owner of the prestigious Townsend Acres Farm here in Lexington, said they've thought all along that the filly had potential, and today's race confirmed their beliefs. They may be considering the Triple Crown for the filly. Of course, Townsend Acres has another extremely promising two-year-old in their stable this year —Townsend Prince, half-brother to Ashleigh's Wonder, and currently favored to win the Breeder's Cup Juvenile in two weeks. . . ."

"I don't believe him!" Ashleigh cried. "The nerve! 'They've thought all along the filly had potential'!" she read in an enraged voice. "Wonder wouldn't have even raced if it had been up to them! Why didn't you say something, Charlie?"

Charlie chuckled at her anger. "What was I supposed to say? It's just words. We got what we wanted —got the filly out on the track showing her stuff."

"It just makes me so mad that Brad's trying to take the credit. You and I did all the work!"

"That's life, missy. The Townsends own the farm

and the filly. They've got the money. They'll say what they want."

Ashleigh knew what he said was true, but the unfairness of it infuriated her. Brad had said so many rotten things about Wonder and had teased Ashleigh frequently.

When she returned from the stables later that afternoon, Caroline was finally awake. She was sitting up in bed, but her hair was standing on end from having lain in bed so long. The skin around her right eye was blackened, but her blue eyes were blazing and sparking like firecrackers. Her left arm was strapped across her chest in a cast. Surrounding her on the bed covers and the floor was a sea of torn and scattered flowers.

"You're awake!" Ashleigh cried. "How do you feel? And what's all this mess?"

Caroline ignored the question about her health. "Do you know what Brad had the *nerve* to send?" she screeched.

"Flowers?" Ashleigh asked weakly, gazing at the disaster in the bedroom.

"Two dozen of them! Mom just brought them up to me. And that's what's left of them!" Caroline made a sweeping gesture with her unbroken right arm.

For an instant Ashleigh thought that the flowers meant Brad was apologizing, or at least feeling sincerely bad about Caro's accident. Unconsciously, she leaned over and started picking up the broken stems.

"Leave them there!" Caroline cried. "I don't want them."

"Why did you throw them around?" Ashleigh asked in confusion. "What did he say?"

"*He* said *nothing*!" Caroline glowered. "The *card* said, 'With our wishes for a speedy recovery, The *Townsends*.' The creep! He hasn't called *once*. He couldn't even send a personal note! His parents did it for him. He's such a piece of slime, Ashleigh! I don't know what I ever saw in him! Well, good-*bye*, Mr. Bradley H. Townsend!"

At Caroline's furious words, Ashleigh couldn't stop herself. She started to giggle.

Caroline sat up straighter in bed. "What are you laughing at?" she said furiously.

"You look so funny—no, really—I'm laughing because I'm so happy that you're finally mad at Brad! Maybe we should pack up this mess and send it back to him in the florist's box."

Caro started to smile. "Great idea!" she said with a wicked gleam in her eye.

"But maybe not." Ashleigh hesitated as she picked up a handful of flower parts. "If his parents sent these on their own, they'd be pretty upset to get them back. The Townsends have always been good to the staff here."

"So? It's time they knew what a slimeball their son is!"

"Do you think they know what happened? That Brad dropped you because he was already going out—" Ashleigh gasped and stopped. She'd said too much.

Caroline's face went white. "You knew!"

"I didn't know for sure. I—I saw him with her at Pimlico, but her father looked like he was talking business with Mr. Townsend." Ashleigh looked down, away from her sister's accusing eyes. "I did see him riding here with her . . . but that was the same day you told me he'd broken up with you, and I didn't want to say anything and make you feel worse."

"Who is she?" Caroline cried.

"I don't know." Ashleigh wanted to crawl away and hide.

Caroline grabbed an untouched daisy from the coverlet, crushed it in her hand, and threw the flower head across the room. Tears started streaming down her cheeks. "He doesn't even wait three days, and he takes *her* to the track. It makes me look like an absolute fool!"

"You're *not* a fool, Caro! And anyway, you're prettier than she is."

"She's rich, isn't she?" Caroline went on angrily. "She'd have to be if her father's doing business with Clay Townsend."

"I don't know."

Caroline didn't seem to be listening anymore. "And I cracked up Mom and Dad's car. . . ." she gasped.

"They're not mad." Ashleigh rushed over to put her arm around Caro's shoulder. "All the stable people were asking for you, hoping you're feeling better."

"Sure . . . they feel sorry for me! Poor Caroline—dumb enough to think the owner's son was interested in her."

"Caroline, stop!" Ashleigh cried.

But Caro flopped back against the mattress and turned her head to the wall. She pulled the sheets up over her face. "Go away. I just want to be alone for a while."

"But Caro—"

"Go away! Leave me alone!"

Ashleigh backed from the room. She didn't know what to say, or what to do to help. As she left the house, she saw her mother coming out of the breeding barn. Ashleigh hurried over.

"What's wrong?" her mother asked.

Ashleigh explained quickly.

"She needs to cry," Mrs. Griffen said, "but I'll go up and talk to her. I know you're upset, Ashleigh, but Caroline needs time to get over the hurt."

As Ashleigh walked up the drive to the stable, she couldn't get her sister's pain out of her mind. She was so preoccupied coming down the barn aisle that she walked straight into Brad Townsend.

"Uh—sorry," she said absently before she realized who it was.

"You ought to watch where you're going," Brad said, straightening. He reached up to hang Townsend Prince's lead shank on the hook outside the horse's stall. "The filly ran a good race yesterday," he added. "A nice surprise. You see the write-up in today's paper?"

"Yes," Ashleigh said coldly.

"I'm glad I was at the track and could talk to the reporters. It's good publicity for the farm. Well, see ya," he said lazily and started down the aisle.

Ashleigh stared at him. Wasn't he even going to ask about her sister? Could he be that much of a creep? Her temper completely snapped. "Aren't you even a *little* bit sorry?" she called after him.

He swung around. "Sorry about what?"

"Caroline! You didn't even bother to ask how she is. She only got in that accident because she saw you at the track with your new girlfriend!"

Brad scowled, then leaned back against the wall between the stalls and stuffed his hands in his jeans pockets. "Caro knew it was over. I made it clear to her."

"Sure—on the phone. And then you embarrassed her in front of all the grooms!"

Brad's mouth tightened. "You ought to mind your

own business, Ashleigh. This hasn't got anything to do with you."

"It does when my sister gets hurt!"

Brad smirked. "Look, your sister made too big a deal out of our dating. I was never that serious. I can't help it that she got hurt. That's the way it goes sometimes. I sent her flowers."

"Your *parents* sent her flowers. You didn't even sign the card. Did you have to rub your new girlfriend in her face—"

Brad cut her short. "I've got better things to do than listen to this!" he said coldly. "You ought to remember who you are. Maybe my father's got a soft spot for you and Charlie, but the rest of us don't. If I have anything to say about it, you and Charlie won't be working with that filly much longer."

Brad quickly strode off. Ashleigh stared at his back. In a moment she heard the powerful engine of his Ferrari, then the squeal of his tires as he roared out of the yard. What had she done? She put her hand to her mouth as Brad's threat slowly sank in.

Ashleigh was trembling when she went into Wonder's stall. Wonder sensed something was wrong. The filly whuffed nervously and stepped across the stall to gently nudge Ashleigh. Ashleigh looked up into the filly's trusting brown eyes and felt her heart sink. *Maybe my father has a soft spot, but the rest of us don't. . . . You and Charlie won't be working with that filly much longer.*

Ashleigh shuddered and threw her arms around Wonder's neck. Maybe he didn't mean it. Maybe he'd only said it to get back at her for yelling at him about Caro. But maybe she'd just given him the excuse he'd needed. Now that Wonder was doing so well, Brad wanted the glory for himself.

Ashleigh laid her cheek against Wonder's silky neck and moaned. "Oh, girl, I think I just made a real *big* mistake!"

8

ASHLEIGH DIDN'T HAVE THE COURAGE TO TELL CHARLIE WHAT she'd done. She dreaded to think what he'd have to say! She did talk to Linda the next morning.

"You're right," Linda said mournfully. "Brad deserved it, but you probably shouldn't have told him off."

"What an absolutely awful weekend this has been!" Ashleigh cried.

"Except for Wonder's race. And at least with the Breeder's Cup, Brad won't be around much the next few weeks," Linda reassured her. "Maybe he'll have forgotten about your argument by the time he gets back."

"I doubt it," Ashleigh groaned.

As soon as Corey saw the girls coming down the hall, she rushed up. Jennifer was right behind her. "Ashleigh, how's Caroline?" Corey exclaimed.

"How'd you know?"

"It was in the paper yesterday. Didn't you see it?"
Ashleigh shook her head.

"Did Caro and Brad really break up?" Jennifer
asked. Her blue eyes were wide with avid curiosity.

"Yeah," Ashleigh said shortly. "News really gets
around fast, doesn't it?"

"I heard about it at the club. Someone said Brad
took Melinda Westwood to the races Saturday."

"Is that her name?" Ashleigh murmured under her
breath.

"So when did they break up?" Jennifer pressed.
"Has he been going out with anyone else?"

Ashleigh had had enough. She slammed her locker
shut. "Find out for yourself, if you're so interested."
She turned her back on Jennifer and strode off angrily
toward homeroom.

Caroline's mood went up and down during the
week while she recuperated. One day all she could
talk about was what a jerk Brad was, and the next,
she looked ready to cry again.

At least Caro's friend Marcy had been coming over
every afternoon to cheer her up. "Marcy told me that
most of the kids at school are on my side," Caroline
told Ashleigh one night. "They think Brad really acted
like a rat. And guess who called me this afternoon?"
she added with a smile. "Justin McGowan."

Ashleigh had heard Caro and Marcy talk about the handsome senior-class president. "Hey, that's great, Caro. Did he ask you out?"

"Not yet . . . but he will."

But Caro fell to pieces again when she saw the Sunday sports pages after the Breeder's Cup races. Ashleigh managed to grab the newspaper before Caro tore it to shreds, and she saw what had made Caro so angry. Townsend Prince had won the Juvenile race, and there was a photo of the horse, with Brad and his new girlfriend standing beside him. The caption under the photo read, ". . . Brad Townsend and Melinda Westwood, daughter of Gerald Westwood of the illustrious Westwood stables, in the winner's circle."

"She *is* rich!" Caroline growled. "That snob thinks he's too good for the breeding managers' daughter!"

The day Ashleigh had been dreading finally arrived. The Townsends were back full-time at the farm. Ashleigh went out of her way to avoid running into Brad, but that wasn't easy.

Charlie had given Wonder a few weeks' rest, but by late November he had Ashleigh start riding the filly over the trails and working her lightly on the oval. Brad was usually somewhere around. Townsend Prince was being given a rest after his big Breeders' Cup effort, but Brad seemed to be taking more of an interest in the other horses in training. He and his father were frequently out by the track in the morning with Maddock and Jennings, watching the horses work.

Ashleigh waited in dread for Brad to turn his threat into action. She still hadn't told Charlie—she didn't dare to admit what she'd done. She began to hope that Brad had forgotten, that he'd only said what he had because he was so angry. His father wasn't likely to take Wonder away from Charlie when the filly was finally doing so well.

Still, Ashleigh cringed every time she saw Brad or Mr. Townsend talking to Charlie. Her guilty secret and her fears for Wonder nagged at her. Her concentration was suffering, too. Whenever Brad watched the morning workouts, she felt herself tensing up. She was so afraid she'd do something wrong that she couldn't relax. Wonder had picked up on Ashleigh's nervousness. The confused filly fidgeted during the workouts on the oval. Her normally smooth strides grew choppy and labored. The more Ashleigh struggled to relax, the more tense she became. She knew she was trying too hard, but she didn't know how to stop.

Finally, after a particularly bad workout, Charlie exploded. The Townsends, Maddock, and Jim Jennings had all been watching. Ashleigh had felt their eyes on her, especially Brad's, and had been a wreck. Wonder came off the oval sweating, even though it was a cold morning.

"What's the matter with you?" Charlie yelled. "You've got the filly tight as a drum! I've never seen you ride so bad! You trying to undo all the good work?"

Ashleigh's face paled with the criticism—especially since Charlie was right. "I'm sorry," she said as she dismounted.

"Sorry's not any excuse!"

Ashleigh stared down at her boots. She didn't know what to say. If she told Charlie why she was so nervous, he'd get even angrier. "I'll try to loosen up," she said meekly.

"No wonder the Townsend kid's been making noises about putting up another rider."

Ashleigh's eyes widened. She stared at Charlie. "Brad?"

Charlie started walking to the barn. Ashleigh quickly followed, leading Wonder.

"Who do you think?" Charlie grouched. "Knew they'd start interfering as soon as they saw what the filly could do—but no point in giving them an excuse! Next they'll be telling me I don't know how to train her!"

Ashleigh was mortified. She had to say something, but the words froze in her throat.

"Take her in the barn and dry her off before you walk her," Charlie growled. He slammed his hat down further on his head—a sure sign he was angry.

Jilly came walking up, leading the horse she'd been working. Ashleigh could see from Jilly's expression that she knew what was going on.

"Ashleigh, maybe you're just too keyed up. It's an easy thing to have happen when you know a horse is doing well."

Ashleigh wished it was that simple. She felt the sting of tears on her eyelids and blinked them away. "I guess . . ." she whispered.

"Let me get this horse to its groom," Jilly said. "I'll be back in a minute. And don't yell at her, Charlie. You'll only make her feel worse."

Charlie grunted disagreeably and stalked ahead into the barn. Ashleigh slowly followed. Her steps were leaden. "I'm sorry, Wonder," she whispered. "I don't know what to do."

Charlie was already waiting at a set of cross-ties with Wonder's halter. He slid it over the filly's head and clipped on the cross-ties as Ashleigh removed Wonder's bridle and saddle. Charlie didn't say a word, but his silence was like a wall of ice. Ashleigh carried the gear to the tack room, then collected a sponge, some clean towels, and a bucket of warm water. She started back down the aisle, then stopped in her tracks.

Clay Townsend was talking to Charlie. His back was toward Ashleigh, but Ashleigh heard him clearly.

"We've all been talking, Charlie," he said. "I know

my son's already mentioned it to you. The filly needs another exercise rider. I know the Griffen girl's put a lot of work into the horse, but it's gotten to the point where she's just not good enough—especially when we're thinking of heading this filly to the big races. You talk to her and explain it. But let's have Jilly work her from now on, and if Jilly's riding at the track, my son or one of the more seasoned riders can handle her."

As Ashleigh listened, she felt a burning flush rise up her neck to her cheeks. Then just as suddenly, she felt terribly cold all over. She set down the pail before she spilled it. She couldn't hear Charlie's response, but she saw Mr. Townsend walk away out of the barn. Jilly was standing a few yards behind Charlie with a look of shock on her face. Thankfully, there weren't any other spectators, since the grooms were either walking horses or had gone to breakfast in the staff's quarters.

In a daze, Ashleigh walked down the aisle toward Charlie. So Brad had carried out his threat. She couldn't believe it had really happened! She wasn't going to be allowed to ride Wonder anymore! It was just about the worst thing anyone could do to her.

Charlie was staring at the floor, shaking his head. In a second he looked up and saw Ashleigh.

"You heard," he said.

"Yes—oh, Charlie—it's all my fault . . . I should have told you . . ." Ashleigh's voice cracked and suddenly the tears came. She stood with clenched fists, tears streaming down her cheeks, staring at Wonder.

Jilly came up and put her hand on Ashleigh's arm. "I'm so sorry, Ash."

"Told me what?" Charlie demanded.

"I had a fight with Brad," Ashleigh stammered. "Right after my sister's accident, I . . . I told him off. He was angry. He said his father was just being soft letting me ride and letting you train her . . ."

Charlie groaned.

Ashleigh stumbled on. ". . . that he and the others weren't so soft—if he had anything to say about it, you and I wouldn't be working with her much longer."

"And you didn't tell me?" Charlie shouted, pulling off his hat and smashing it between his hands.

"I was afraid you'd yell at me."

"At least I'd have been prepared! I suppose all this has something to do with the way you've been riding lately?"

Ashleigh flinched at Charlie's tone. "I couldn't concentrate. I get so nervous when they're watching—"

"If I'd know what was wrong, I could have helped you out. One of the first rules in this business is you *never* insult an owner—not if you want to keep training a horse and making a living!"

"Charlie," Jilly said quickly, "she had a good reason

for it. He's a spoiled brat, and you know what he did to Caroline."

"He could be the devil himself, and you *still* don't tell him what you think!" Charlie slammed his hat back on his head and scowled. "All right," he said in a moment. "I can see you losing your temper. But if you'd told me, I would have been prepared to deal with it. Now we really got some problems! I'll be darned if I'll let that Townsend kid get on the filly's back. I don't like the way he rides."

At the mention of Brad riding, Ashleigh closed her eyes in pain. That suggestion of Mr. Townsend's had been the biggest blow of all.

"Shh," Jilly said, motioning with her head to the end of the barn. A groom had just entered, leading in a horse. "Anyway, let's not worry about that yet. I'll be around for a while to ride her. Maddock won't be sending me to any races until January."

"You never know."

Ashleigh bit her lip. "I've really blown it. I thought maybe Brad would forget about the fight. But I guess now that Wonder's doing so well, he's just looking for a chance to take over. Oh, Charlie, I didn't mean to mess up your chances, too. And Wonder's." Near tears again, Ashleigh walked over to the filly and pressed her forehead against the horse's neck. Wonder whoofed gently against Ashleigh's dark hair.

Charlie straightened his shoulders. "Well, there's

nothing gained by crying over spilled milk. If we put our heads together, we ought to be able to come up with some plan to put a stop to this."

Ashleigh didn't tell Caroline what had happened. Her sister was finally getting over Brad, and Ashleigh didn't want to upset her. Caro never went anywhere around the farm where she might run into Brad, but she was starting to get involved in new things at school, and had been dating Justin McGowan. Ashleigh suspected that Caroline would blame herself if she found out the problems Ashleigh's argument had caused.

Thank goodness I have Linda to confide in, Ashleigh thought.

"What are you going to do?" Linda gulped when Ashleigh told her about it at school. "How could they do such a rotten thing? I mean, you've done everything for Wonder—everything! They can't just cut you out of the picture!"

"I'm still grooming her." At Linda's sympathy, Ashleigh felt a painful lump in her throat. "And Jilly's riding her for now, which is almost as good as me riding her."

Linda gritted her teeth. "I'd like to wring Brad Townsend's neck."

Wonder didn't seem to realize anything was wrong. Ashleigh was still with her every morning and afternoon, and the filly was used to Jilly riding her. But Ashleigh ached every time she watched the morning workouts, hating herself for blowing her chances. At least Wonder was back in form again, with the prospect of racing in January, and during the cold December days Ashleigh saw Mr. Townsend and Mr. Maddock smile as they watched the filly work.

Then, just before Christmas, Jilly came down with the flu. She came out to the barn to ride at five in the morning anyway, but Charlie took one look at her feverish face and sent her back to bed.

"Charlie," Jilly pleaded, "if I don't ride her, they'll put someone else up on her."

"You're shivering like a leaf," the old man said. "I'm not letting you go out there like that. Wouldn't do anybody any good. Don't worry. If they ask, I'll just tell 'em that I decided to rest her for a day. It's not like we're in heavy training for an upcoming race. I'm not entering her in anything until the end of January."

Jilly was too sick and weak to protest. "All right. Bed sounds awfully good right now. I'll be better tomorrow."

"If you're not, don't drag yourself out here."

When Ashleigh got home from school that afternoon, Charlie told her there'd been no comments about Wonder's not working that day. Ashleigh relaxed, and after she'd groomed Wonder, she went up to Jilly's small apartment in the staff dormitory to see how the apprentice jockey was feeling.

"Come in," Jilly called in answer to Ashleigh's knock. Jilly was dressed, but she was curled up in a chair and wrapped in layers of blankets.

"Feeling any better?" Ashleigh asked.

"Not great," Jilly answered with a sniffle.

"Have you eaten anything? I could make you some soup or something."

"Oh, that would be great, if you don't mind," Jilly said. "There's some canned soup in the cabinet."

Ashleigh went into the tiny kitchen and found the soup and a pan. When it was hot, she poured the steaming liquid into a mug and brought it to Jilly.

"Thanks," Jilly said gratefully, taking a sip and sighing at the warmth. "I feel so cold all the time."

"Charlie said no one mentioned Wonder's not working this morning," Ashleigh told her.

"That's good," Jilly answered, "but you'd better tell Charlie that Maddock stopped by here this afternoon. He knows I'm sick. I told him I'd be ready to ride tomorrow, but I don't think he believed me." Jilly made a face. "Not surprising when I was sitting here burning up with a fever."

Ashleigh's heart sank at the news. She spent another half hour with Jilly and convinced the older girl to get into a warm nightgown and go to bed. She left the rest of the soup by Jilly's bedside, together with a glass and a pitcher of water. "You sure you're going to be okay?" she said to Jilly before she left.

"I only need a good sleep," Jilly mumbled.

"I'll check in later."

Ashleigh stopped by Charlie's rooms on her way back to the house. When he came to the door, she told him about Maddock seeing Jilly. He frowned at the news, but nodded.

"She's pretty sick, Charlie," Ashleigh added. "I'm worried about her."

"Don't fret. I'll keep an eye on her."

Ashleigh slept later than usual the next morning. She'd had so much homework, she'd nearly fallen asleep at the desk the night before and had forgotten to set her alarm.

She rushed through her dressing, careful not to wake her sister, who wouldn't get up for another hour. Then she hurried downstairs, put on her down jacket, and went out into the chill. The ground crunched under her feet, and the frigid dawn air stung her eyes.

Wonder was waiting for her breakfast and whinnied eagerly as Ashleigh approached her stall with fresh hay and water. "It's a cold one today, girl. Everything's frozen out there," Ashleigh said. "I don't think we'll have to worry about you working. Hey, don't be so greedy," Ashleigh scolded as Wonder tore a mouthful of hay from the bundle in Ashleigh's arms. "At least wait till I get the hay in the net."

As Wonder ate, Charlie came to the stall door. "How's Jilly?" Ashleigh asked.

"I'd say she's going to be in bed a couple days," the old man said. "Too cold to work the horses anyway, though I saw Maddock headed out to the oval."

A moment later someone strode up the barn aisle. Ashleigh glanced over the stall door and saw Brad stop outside.

"Saddle her up, Charlie," he said. "I'll take her out today."

"Says who?" Charlie answered. "It's too cold. The ground's frozen. I'm not risking the filly."

"Maddock said the track's okay. He had them run the harrow over it. He's already working a couple of horses, and the filly didn't get worked yesterday."

"Two days off aren't going to hurt her. You know as well as I do she's not racing for another month."

"I'm taking her out, Charlie," Brad snapped. "You can check with my father if you don't believe me."

"It's nuts!" Charlie barked. "The filly's fit. She doesn't need the workout today!"

"I want to see for myself how she's handling now." Brad took Wonder's lead rope from its hook, stepped into the stall, clipped it to her halter, and started leading her out. "Get her tack for me," he said to Ashleigh.

Ashleigh gave Charlie a desperate look. He was fuming, too. His eyes were narrowed and his mouth set, but he shrugged as if to say, "Nothing we can do."

Ashleigh clenched her teeth in fury as she went to the tack room and collected Wonder's gear, cursing Brad under her breath. She knew she had to keep her mouth shut this time, though.

Brad tacked up Wonder himself. He must have known he wouldn't get much cooperation from Ashleigh or Charlie.

"If you're set on working her, then work her light," Charlie ordered. "I don't care if Maddock is working his horses, the ground's hard. I don't want her breezing."

Brad was barely listening. "I know how to ride," he said coldly.

Wonder snorted uneasily, confused to have a stranger handling her. She turned her head and looked nervously at Ashleigh. Ashleigh patted the filly's rump, but there was nothing she could do as Brad led Wonder out of the barn toward the oval.

"I don't believe it," Ashleigh muttered hoarsely to Charlie. "Do you really think his father told him to take her out?"

Charlie nodded. "Townsend's got a blind spot where his son's concerned. I don't know if I've got the heart to watch this. The kid isn't going to listen to me, but I've gotta be out there. You coming?"

Ashleigh couldn't stand the thought of watching Brad ride Wonder. Yet she couldn't bear to desert Wonder, either. She checked her watch—fifteen minutes before she had to leave to catch the bus. Ashleigh followed Charlie.

Ken Maddock was standing by the gate to the track. Mr. Townsend was beside him. Charlie strode over to the two men while Ashleigh went to stand by the rail several yards away, her eyes on Wonder and Brad. The filly was showing her usual morning high spirits, but she was terribly unsettled by the new rider on her back. She toe-danced across the track as Brad tried to get her going, tossing her head and snorting out misting breaths in the cold air. Brad frowned in concentration and held his legs tight on the filly, trying to master her.

Charlie returned, looking more dour than ever.

"What did they say?" Ashleigh asked.

"Neither of them can see how it would hurt her. They agreed she should only get a light gallop, but the kid doesn't have the right touch. Look at him—trying to muscle her around!"

Ashleigh had already seen, and it made her sick. "He's not carrying a whip, anyway."

"None of them are *that* dumb," Charlie grumbled.

Brad finally had Wonder going at a canter, but the filly was tense. She wasn't relaxing as Brad urged her along the backstretch, then around past Charlie and Ashleigh. As they lapped the track again, he pushed Wonder into a gallop.

"I don't like the looks of the track," Charlie mumbled. "Too hard."

Wonder was galloping now, yet her strides seemed choppy. Her mind wasn't on what she was doing, but Brad kept at her. Then suddenly Wonder jumped into a faster pace.

"What's he doing?" Charlie cried.

Ashleigh could see a look of grim satisfaction on Brad's face. Then Wonder stumbled. Her front legs seemed to fold under her. Valiantly, she caught herself and got three legs beneath her, but Brad was nearly thrown from the saddle. He caught himself, grabbing Wonder's mane. Ashleigh felt the blood drain from her face. The filly dropped back into a stumbling trot, then a walk. Ashleigh gasped as Wonder limped forward. She couldn't put any weight on her right foreleg!

Ashleigh had never seen Charlie move so fast. In an instant, he was under the rail and jogging across the track to the filly. Ashleigh was right behind. Brad had already dismounted and was kneeling down by the filly's right fore, examining her ankle and lower leg. Charlie raced up beside him and pushed through to do his own examination. Ashleigh quickly went to Wonder's head, taking the reins and trying to soothe the filly, who grunted in distress. Brad's face had paled, and he looked stunned and frightened.

Ken Maddock and Mr. Townsend rushed up with grim and worried expressions.

"How's it look, Charlie?" Ashleigh whispered fearfully.

"Can't tell for sure till we get some X-rays. No obvious breaks, thank heavens. No heat in the ankle yet. Could be a fracture, or bruised or torn ligaments."

"What happened?" Mr. Townsend asked Brad.

"I'm not sure," Brad answered. "It felt like she took a misstep, but before I could pull her up, she stumbled."

"You were pushing her too fast," Maddock said.

"She wasn't listening," Brad exclaimed. "I had to give her a firm ride."

"Looks like it was a little too firm," his father said harshly. "Think she can get back to the barn on her own?" he asked Charlie.

"We can try," Charlie said.

"I'll go call the vet," Maddock offered. He ran off toward the stable office.

Ashleigh slowly led the hobbling filly forward.

9

DR. JAMES FINALLY ROSE, FINISHING HIS EXAMINATION. "I'LL let you know for sure when I develop the X-rays," he said to Charlie and Clay Townsend. "There may be a slight fracture, but it looks more like bruising and a severely pulled shoulder muscle. You're lucky. Keep her quiet, with her leg packed in ice, and put a compress on her shoulder. I'll call back with the X-ray results and stop by this afternoon to see how she's doing."

Mr. Townsend followed the vet and motioned for Brad to come with him. Gradually the others filed away, leaving Charlie and Ashleigh alone with Wonder. Ashleigh had asked one of the grooms to run down and tell her parents what had happened—she wasn't about to leave Wonder now to go to school, and she hoped her parents would understand. The injury could affect Wonder's whole future.

She and Charlie worked in depressed silence. First they positioned Wonder in cross-ties in her stall, so that she could move around as little as possible. Then they filled a large bucket with ice water and carefully inserted Wonder's injured leg into the liquid. Charlie then made up a compress for her shoulder. The filly didn't seem in obvious pain unless she moved her right shoulder.

About an hour later, Mr. Townsend returned and spoke quietly to Charlie. "I just got a call from Dr. James. No fractures or chips, thank heavens. He says to keep up with the ice pack and compresses." He paused. "But it looks like this puts back our plans for her. She'll have to stay out of training for a while. I'm sorry, Charlie, I should have listened to you about working her today. You think there's still a chance of having her ready for the Triple Crown?"

Charlie pushed back his hat and scratched his head. "We'll have to see how she heals up. She's spunky and in top fit otherwise. She'll mend faster than some, but who knows?"

"I'll leave it to you," Townsend said.

Ashleigh's parents took a few minutes from their busy schedule to stop by Wonder's stall. They tried to reassure Ashleigh and boost her lagging spirits, but they knew what a horrible disappointment Wonder's injury was. Even Rory was subdued when Caroline brought him by after school.

It was the first time Caro had made an appearance in the stables since Brad had broken up with her. Ashleigh wondered if it meant her sister was finally getting over her hurt.

Rory pulled a carrot from his pocket and fed it to Wonder. "You're going to be okay soon, Wonder. You've got to win some big races for Ashleigh."

"I'm really sorry, Ash," Caroline said, reaching in over the stall door and patting Wonder's nose. "It was Brad's fault, wasn't it?"

"Charlie didn't want her to go out at all this morning," Ashleigh said. "It wouldn't have been so bad if Brad hadn't pushed her. But actually, I don't think Brad's feeling too hot right now, either. I heard his father talking to him after we got her back to the stable. Mr. Townsend wasn't happy. And Brad hasn't been around yet this afternoon."

"Afraid to show his face," Caroline said. "Maybe he's finally learned a lesson."

Ashleigh just shrugged. She was beyond anger. It was all so discouraging.

"I thought I'd go over and see how Jilly's doing," Caroline said. "Does she know?"

"The way news gets around here, probably."

* * *

104

Wonder seemed more comfortable by that evening. When Charlie checked Wonder's leg, there was no swelling or heat, but the horse's ankle was obviously sore to the touch.

"I'll spend the night in the stable—keep an eye on her," he told Ashleigh.

"Thanks, Charlie," Ashleigh said.

By morning Wonder's leg still showed no signs of swelling, but she grunted in discomfort when she flexed her shoulder muscles. "She seems more sore than yesterday," Ashleigh worried.

"The muscle's stiffened up with her just standing in one place. But I don't think we need the ice bucket today. She can move around a little more, and I'll start massaging her shoulder."

"Charlie doesn't think there's any way she'll be ready to race this winter," Ashleigh told Linda at lunch. "March will be the earliest, if we're lucky." She toyed with the food on her plate. She'd lost her appetite.

"That doesn't give you much time to prep her for the Derby," Linda sympathized. "What a bummer. Brad really knows how to mess things up."

"Hi, guys!"

They looked up as Corey and Jennifer appeared with their lunch trays and sat down at the table. "Jennifer and I are going to the mall after school to do some Christmas shopping," Corey said. "You two wanna come?"

"Sounds good," Linda answered. "I still need to get a present for my parents."

But Ashleigh shook her head. "I can't today. Wonder was hurt in her workout yesterday morning. I've got to keep an eye on her."

"Hurt?" Corey said. "What happened?"

"She stumbled—pulled her shoulder and bruised her ankle badly."

"Brad was riding her," Linda put in grimly.

Jennifer leaned forward. "Brad?"

"Why was he riding her?" Corey asked. "Where was Jilly?"

"Sick. Brad decided he'd ride, even though Charlie didn't want him to take her out."

"Well, she *is* the Townsends' horse," Jennifer said, tossing her honey-colored hair. "When I talked to Brad at the club, he told me he and his father were going to start taking a bigger interest in her training."

Corey snorted. "Jennifer, be real. Ashleigh raised the horse, and she and Charlie trained her! What's Brad doing sticking his nose in now?"

Ashleigh hid her grin, silently thanking Corey. But Jennifer glared at the other girl. "You're just being a pain because you've decided you shouldn't have broken up with Bobby."

"You broke up with Bobby?" Linda and Ashleigh exclaimed.

"He was flirting around, and I got sick of it."

"Sure, Corey," Jennifer smiled. "That's a good excuse."

"Oh, get lost!" Corey snapped. "I notice Brad hasn't asked you out, like you were hoping."

"He's been busy."

"Right," Corey answered, "with Melinda Westwood."

Jennifer pushed back her chair and stalked off to another table.

"Uh oh," Linda said.

Corey shrugged. "She'll live. At least your sister's gotten over Brad," she added to Ashleigh. "I hear she's going out with Justin McGowan."

Ashleigh nodded. "She seems a lot better. She even came out to the stable yesterday."

For the rest of the lunch period they talked about their plans for the upcoming Christmas vacation. Linda was traveling to Virginia with her father to pick up some new stock, and Corey was going north on a skiing trip with her family. Ashleigh would be spending her time nursing Wonder, instead of training her as she'd expected.

But at home, Rory was excited about Christmas, even if Ashleigh wasn't. He asked Ashleigh's help in putting together a stocking for his favorite weanling, whom he'd named Lightning. It was a tradition Ashleigh had started when Wonder was a weanling. Despite herself, Ashleigh caught some of her brother's enthusiasm for the holiday. Together they filled stockings for Lightning, Wonder, and Wonder's dam, Holly, then went out to the stables to hang them outside each stall.

Ashleigh had gone to the mall with Caro to do her shopping, and the two of them chipped in on a present for their parents—a new radio for their office. Caro had gotten her arm cast off weeks before, and had finally ventured to drive again. The two girls locked themselves in their room to do their wrapping.

Christmas day was a happy time, with the family opening gifts around the tree and Charlie and Jilly joining them later for Christmas dinner. For a few hours everyone was able to put aside their worries.

Ashleigh didn't see much of Brad as she tended to Wonder during vacation week. He seemed to be avoiding her now, which didn't bother Ashleigh in the least. She only hoped he was so embarrassed that he'd stop interfering with Wonder altogether.

Brad had Townsend Prince to keep him busy, anyway. As of the first of January, Townsend Prince and Wonder officially turned three. Townsend Prince was in full training for his three-year-old season, and would soon be shipped to Florida to prepare for the big winter races. Wonder would spend the next weeks in her stall and wouldn't even be able to begin training for another month at least.

Each time Ashleigh saw Brad riding Townsend Prince to or from the training oval, her anger burned again. Brad's colt was fit and strong and ready to go, while poor Wonder limped around, with her three-year-old future uncertain—all because of Brad!

Townsend Prince was shipped out to Florida in mid-January and won the Tropical Park Derby, adding more shine to his already brilliant star. The racing reporters and handicappers saw the colt as the standout favorite for the Derby in early May. Reading about Townsend Prince's success only made Ashleigh more restless and moody.

"Come on, look at the good side!" Linda scolded Ashleigh one January afternoon. They'd gone over to Linda's to do their homework and were both sprawled across Linda's bed. "Charlie said Wonder's improving faster than he expected. If she can get back into training in February, she'll still have a chance to run in some prep races. Look, here's the Derby prep schedule from the paper." Linda spread out the clipping from the *Lexington Herald.* "There's the Florida Derby in March. You could point her at that."

"No good," Ashleigh said. "Townsend Prince is running, and the field will be all colts. Wonder won't be ready for that kind of competition after such a long layoff."

Linda wouldn't give up. She ran her finger down the list of races. "Hmm. How about the Tampa Bay Derby? That's later in the month, and it probably won't draw such a big field. You don't think they'd send her to California?"

Ashleigh shook her head. "Charlie said Mr. Townsend had already decided to stick to the East Coast prep races."

"Well, there's the Jim Beam at Turfway at the end of March, and there's always the Blue Grass at Keeneland, and the prep races in New York and New Jersey in April."

Ashleigh finally smiled. "Okay, I get the message. I shouldn't give up."

"You need to do something besides worry about Wonder. There's the big basketball game at the high school Friday night," Linda added. "Why don't you come with me?"

"Oh, right, Caroline was talking about it. If Henry Clay wins, they go to the state finals. Caroline's going with Marcy. Maybe they can give us a ride."

Linda smiled, satisfied.

But, despite Linda's optimism, Ashleigh couldn't help feeling frustrated. It was nearly the end of January, and although Charlie was having Ashleigh take Wonder for longer and longer walks, leading her at a trot now, he still wouldn't make any commitments about when Wonder could start seriously training again. The filly's bruised ankle was healed, but Charlie was concerned about her pulled shoulder muscles.

"The worst thing we can do," he told Ashleigh, "is put her back into heavy training before she's one hundred percent fit." Ashleigh agreed, but she'd never had a lot of patience.

On Friday night Ashleigh and Caroline climbed into Marcy's car and headed out to pick up Linda for the basketball game. The Griffen's car was repaired, but Caroline was still nervous about driving.

The Henry Clay basketball team was having one of the best seasons in its history, and the bleachers of the gym were overflowing with spectators. Caroline and Marcy went off to sit with Justin and some other friends. Ashleigh and Linda soon spotted Corey, Jennifer, and some kids from their class and sat with them.

The action in the first half was intense. Ashleigh screamed at the top of her lungs with the rest of the fans as the teams raced back and forth across the court, scoring alternating baskets.

By the halftime break, as the cheerleaders paraded in front of the stands, Ashleigh felt hoarse. She turned to talk to Linda, then she heard someone speak to her from her other side.

"You're Caroline Griffen's sister, aren't you?"

Ashleigh looked over at a dark-haired boy sitting on

the bleacher next to her. She didn't recognize him, but she nodded.

"I'm Chad McGowan, Justin's brother," he explained. "Your sister was telling me about the filly you've trained. I saw her last race at Keeneland. Great effort."

Ashleigh smiled. "Yeah, we thought so. You heard she's been laid up with an injury, though."

"Yeah. Sorry to hear that. By the way," he motioned to the blond boy sitting next to him, "this is my friend, Mike Reese. Mike, Ashleigh Griffen. Mike and I are training a couple of two-year-olds together, and we've got three good yearlings coming on."

"Really?" Ashleigh said. She shifted in her seat. He had her complete interest now. "Caro didn't say anything about your family being in the racing business."

"No, but my family is," Mike Reese answered. "We have a small place over near Versailles, Whitebrook Farm. My father bought it a couple of years ago, and we're still building up the business. He was a trainer for one of the big outfits in Florida before we came up here."

"Are you breeding, or just training?" Ashleigh asked.

"We're starting a breeding operation. One of our stallions was bred at Townsend Acres. His dam's Mischief Maiden, and he's out of Barbero."

Ashleigh recognized the names of the mare and stallion still housed at Townsend Acres. Mischief Maiden was Three-Foot's official name, and Three-Foot was Townsend Prince's dam.

"We got him at auction as a two-year-old—cheap," Mike continued with a smile. "So when do you think Wonder will go back in training? I read that the Townsends were thinking of aiming her toward the Derby."

Ashleigh frowned. "I'm not sure what's going to happen now. She's healing well, but Charlie wants to wait till she's a hundred percent—you know Charlie Burke, who's been training her?"

"I know who he is and his reputation. We'd love to pick up some tips from that old guy."

Ashleigh laughed. "Charlie'd like hearing that!"

For the rest of halftime, the three of them talked about the technicalities of training, the quirks of their own horses, and of the upcoming racing season. It wasn't until the game resumed that Ashleigh realized how engrossed she'd been in their conversation.

Linda jabbed her with her elbow.

"What? Why are you looking at me like that?" Ashleigh asked when she saw Linda's expression. Jennifer and Corey were staring at her, too.

"I'll tell you later," Linda whispered.

The action in the second half of the game had everyone sitting on the edge of their seats, jumping up when Henry Clay scored, groaning when the opposition did. The two teams were still only a few points apart, with Henry Clay down by two, and the clock was ticking away. Henry Clay took aggressive action, scoring from center court and not letting the other team have the ball. The buzzer sounded, ending the game, and the fans went wild.

Ashleigh and Linda jumped to their feet with everyone else. But before they all filed off the bleachers, Mike leaned over and spoke to Ashleigh over the din. "Chad and I would love to take a look at your filly sometime and meet Charlie. Mind if I give you a call?"

"No, fine. I'll give you and Chad a tour of the farm."

"Hey, great. Thanks. See ya."

" 'Bye." Ashleigh smiled as she headed down the bleachers.

Linda could barely wait to get her alone. She pulled Ashleigh aside as they left the gym.

"Do you know those guys that you were talking to?" Linda exclaimed.

"Sure," Ashleigh shrugged. "Chad McGowan and Mike Reese."

"What were you talking about for so long?"

"Horses—they're training some together, and they liked Wonder's last race."

"Oh, my God," Linda groaned. "You really don't know who they are, do you?"

Ashleigh sighed in exasperation. "I just *told* you!"

"No, I mean, how popular they are—how many

girls are *dying* to go out with them. Didn't you see Jennifer and Corey staring at you?"

"I thought they were giving me funny looks. Why?"

"They were jealous, dummy!" Linda cried. "Ashleigh, sometimes—no, most of the time—I think you walk around with a bag on your head. I mean, I know you're more interested in Wonder right now than dating, but can you really be that dumb?"

"I don't know what you're yelling at me for!" Ashleigh said, angry at Linda's tone. "Just because I don't start drooling and acting like a ninny because a couple of guys talk to me—"

"All through halftime?" Linda yelped.

"We were talking *horses* !"

"I heard what Mike said to you when the game was over—so did Jennifer and Corey. He asked if he could call you!"

"Yeah, they want to see Wonder and talk to Charlie."

Linda groaned again and threw up her hands. "You're hopeless. I know where Jennifer will be tomorrow morning—at the library, reading every book on horse training she can get her hands on."

Ashleigh chuckled at the thought. "She probably already did that when she got interested in Brad. It didn't do her much good. Come on, let's find Caro and Marcy or we won't get a ride home."

10

"ALL I GOT FROM JENNIFER BEFORE ENGLISH WERE QUESTIONS about why Chad McGowan and Mike Reese were talking to you," Linda said when she met Ashleigh at her locker after school on Monday. "She was absolutely dying to know if Mike called you over the weekend. She and Corey are trying to decide if he's going to ask you out."

Ashleigh laughed. "Me? That's hysterical! I've never even had a date, and I don't want to."

"Come on, Ash, dating's not that bad. I had fun when I went out with Seth Hoffman—even if we're really just friends. And, heck, you're nearly fifteen. A lot of kids think it's weird that all you're interested in is horses —that you never go out with anyone. It's not like you're ugly or anything."

"Thanks." Ashleigh scowled. "Why don't they just mind their own business? What's wrong with being interested in horses? I *like* it. It's important to me! I have more fun with Wonder than I would with any of the guys I know. Would you rather I turned into an airhead like Jennifer?"

"You know that's not what I meant—and you don't have to get so mad."

"Look at the mess Caro was in over Brad!" Ashleigh rushed on. "I'm not going to go around crying over some jerk."

"Not all guys are idiots like Brad," Linda began, then she shrugged. "Never mind . . . forget I said anything."

The next day Charlie decided that Wonder should start back in training. He started her on the longe line, trotting and cantering her in a circle to limber her up. By the end of the week he was satisfied enough to tell Ashleigh and Jilly that they'd start taking her out on the trails.

Ashleigh took out Dominator, and Charlie saddled Belle. Ashleigh ached with longing to be in Wonder's saddle, but at least with Jilly riding, Ashleigh had a chance to watch Wonder from a distance—to see the fluid movements that she could only feel when she was on Wonder's back. Jilly rode superbly—there was no question of that. But whenever Ashleigh saw Brad in the stable yard, she was reminded that he was partially responsible for her not being able to ride.

Fortunately, he stayed away from her, and if they

did accidentally pass in the aisle, they merely nodded to each other and kept walking.

By the end of another week, Wonder was regaining full condition, and Charlie was pleased. "We'll keep up these distance rides a little longer," he said. "She's coming back in form, but she's going to have to keep running longer distances if we head her to the Triple Crown."

"No one's said anything about my riding her again, have they?" Ashleigh asked.

"Nope," Charlie answered. "Don't expect that they will. Why? You think you're ready to ride again?"

"At least on the trails," Ashleigh said. "I really messed up last fall, but you know why I was riding so badly. I won't be so nervous now."

Charlie grunted, but said no more.

Yet when Ashleigh arrived in the stables the following afternoon, Charlie had only Wonder and Belle saddled. "Get up on her," he said to Ashleigh, motioning with his head to Wonder.

"You mean it?" Ashleigh gasped.

"For the trail ride today, anyway. Jilly had to go into town."

"Does Mr. Townsend know?"

"We had a talk about the filly this morning. I'll start her back on the oval the end of the week, and if she looks okay, I'll see about sending her down to Florida in a month."

Ashleigh didn't press the old trainer for details. It was enough that she would be riding Wonder again— at least for one day. Her face glowed as she settled herself in the saddle. She leaned over Wonder's neck and whispered to the filly, "We're a team again, girl. How about that?"

Wonder whickered contentedly and playfully tossed her head.

"Okay, let's go," Charlie said. "None of this sentimental stuff."

Their ride was perfect, and Ashleigh knew without being told that she'd ridden at her best. Charlie seemed quietly satisfied as they rode back into the stable yard. Terry Bush and Hank were outside, and both of them grinned in surprise to see Ashleigh in Wonder's saddle. Terry flashed her the thumbs up sign and called, "Glad to see you back up there."

Ashleigh was glowing with happiness when she went home for dinner. There were going to be a lot of tense days ahead, getting Wonder ready to return to racing, but at least Ashleigh really felt a part of it again.

Just after the family finished eating, Ashleigh got a phone call. She figured it was Linda and answered breezily when her father handed her the receiver. "I've got the greatest news!"

There was a moment's silence, then a male voice said, "Is that Ashleigh?"

Ashleigh swallowed in surprise. "Yes."

"Hi, it's Mike Reese. Hope the good news is about your filly."

"Oh—hi." Ashleigh had almost forgotten about Mike's promise to call. For a second she felt tongue-tied. Then she pulled herself together. "Yes, it was. It looks like she'll be ready to start galloping by the end of the week."

"The more I read about the other Derby hopefuls, the more I'd like to see Wonder get out there and beat the heck out of them."

Ashleigh laughed. Mike's tone was easy and friendly, and she began to relax. "Yeah, me, too. How're your two-year-olds doing?"

"We can't complain, although we're not looking to race them until late spring. Listen, I was wondering if Chad and I could take you up on that offer to see the filly? But maybe this isn't a good time, now that she's back in heavy training."

Ashleigh hesitated, thinking of schedules. "Well, maybe Saturday afternoon. We usually finish the work fairly early on the weekend."

"That'd be great! Thanks. You think Charlie would mind if Chad and I picked his brains?"

"Well, you can try." Ashleigh smiled. "Just don't expect too much. Charlie's not much of a talker."

"Around three okay?" Mike asked.

"Sure. Fine."

"See you then."

When Ashleigh hung up the phone and turned, she saw her sister watching her from across the kitchen with a cat-who-ate-the-canary grin. "Was that who I think it was?" Caroline asked.

"I don't know," Ashleigh said unhelpfully, but she felt her cheeks flushing under Caroline and her mother's gaze.

"It was Mike Reese, wasn't it?" Caroline didn't wait for Ashleigh to confirm it. "Justin told me he was going to call. So he's coming over Saturday, huh?"

"With Chad. They want to look at the filly and to talk to Charlie."

"Sure," Caroline said with a sly smile. Ashleigh's mother was smiling, too.

"I don't know what you're all grinning about!" Ashleigh snapped. "He's not coming over to see me."

"Wanna bet?" Caroline said.

Rory looked up from the arithmetic problems he was doing at the kitchen table. "You finally have a date, Ashleigh?"

"No!" She couldn't believe it—even Rory was starting in on her! "They're training horses of their own and just want a look at what we're doing here. I don't know what's the matter with all of you." Quickly Ashleigh turned her back on the grinning trio and left the room.

After the way her family had reacted, Ashleigh

wasn't about to tell Linda that Mike and Chad were coming over. By now everyone at school had forgotten about Ashleigh's conversation at the basketball game, and Ashleigh didn't want to start the gossip going again.

Promptly at three on Saturday a small pickup truck pulled up in the stable yard. Ashleigh had been waiting just inside the first stable building, having last-minute doubts about telling Mike and Chad to come. Not until they'd exchanged friendly greetings was Ashleigh able to relax a little and put Caroline's teasing from her mind. Especially when Mike's first comment was, "Well, let's see that filly of yours."

"She's down here. I just finished grooming her," Ashleigh said, leading Mike and Chad down the barn aisle.

Wonder pranced elegantly across her stall, putting on a show for her admirers.

"She knows when she's got an audience," Ashleigh smiled, opening the stall. "Come on in. She's easygoing unless she takes a dislike to someone."

"So you think she likes us, huh?" Chad asked with a grin.

Ashleigh held Wonder's head as the two boys admired and discussed Wonder's conformation.

"She's not awfully big," Chad said, "but nice and compact. Beautiful animal."

"You can sure see her breeding," Mike added. "I'd

love to get some Townsend Pride blood into our stable."

"Why don't you?" Ashleigh asked. "They breed him to outside mares."

"We couldn't afford the stud fees—they're up to twenty thousand this year. Besides, Townsend's pretty choosy about who he'll breed him to."

"You might have gotten Wonder pretty cheap two years ago," Ashleigh said sourly. "They nearly sent her to auction as a yearling."

"Well, we would have loved it," Mike said. "But the Townsends would have been making a big mistake. They're sure not sorry they've got her now."

"No, not now," Ashleigh agreed.

Over the next hour, Ashleigh relaxed further. Mike and Chad were serious and knowledgeable horsemen, and the conversation was strictly horses and training. As they returned from looking at the stallions, the training oval, and the yearling walking ring, they found Charlie coming out of his rooms. Ashleigh motioned to him and introduced Mike and Chad.

To her surprise, Charlie immediately took a liking to the two young men. He seemed glad to talk about his favorite training techniques and the many horses he'd trained over the years. He was interested, too, in what Mike and Chad were doing, and talked to Mike at length about bloodlines and the breeding stock Mike's father was acquiring.

Ashleigh leaned back against one of the trees in the stable yard and listened intently, totally forgetting herself. Soon she was surprised to realize that dusk was falling and the February air had suddenly grown much colder.

Mike and Chad seemed to realize this, too. They said their good-byes to Charlie, thanking him, and invited him to take a look at their horses.

"Maybe I will," Charlie said, "if Jilly can give me a ride over sometime."

"I'll pick you up," Mike said. "You'd be doing us a favor."

Ashleigh walked back to the truck with them. After Mike climbed into the driver's seat, he rolled down the window and leaned his head out. "Incredible afternoon," he said to Ashleigh. "Thanks. We learned a lot."

Ashleigh returned his smile. Chad and Mike waved, and the truck drew off. Ashleigh went into the stables and caught up with Charlie, who was heading to Wonder's stall. "I hope you didn't mind them asking you all those questions," she said.

"Nope. Nice boys. Got heads on their shoulders. Think I just might go take a look at what they're bringing along."

Ashleigh had barely set foot in the house when Caroline popped her head out from the living room. "So? Tell me everything!"

"There isn't anything to tell, Caro," Ashleigh sighed. "I took them around. They liked what they saw, and thought Wonder looked good. Then they talked to Charlie."

"Ashleigh, that isn't all!" Caroline exclaimed, laughing. "I saw the way Mike was looking at you."

"What do you mean—you saw?"

Caroline flushed. "Well, Rory and I were taking a walk and we sort of ended up near the stables—"

"You sneak! And besides, he wasn't looking at *me* ."

"That's what you think!" Caroline laughed again, then she glanced at her watch. "Is it that late already? I've got to go take a shower. I'm going out with Justin tonight."

Ashleigh had a dentist appointment after school on Tuesday and wasn't home when Mike came to drive Charlie to Whitebrook. Ashleigh wouldn't have known Charlie had gone if Jilly hadn't mentioned it the next morning as they were getting ready to go out to the oval with Wonder.

"Who did Charlie go off with yesterday?" she asked. "He said something about it being a friend of yours. I saw them when they were leaving. The guy who picked him up was cute, tall, and blond, and driving a pickup."

"It must have been Mike Reese," Ashleigh said,

explaining to Jilly about Chad and Mike. "Charlie didn't tell me he was going."

"He needs to get off the farm once in a while," Jilly said. "He seemed pretty cheerful this morning—for Charlie anyway. He must have had a good time."

11

ON A BRISK SATURDAY MORNING IN EARLY MARCH, ASHLEIGH watched the van carrying Wonder move off down the drive en route to Florida. She'd been so excited about the prospect of Wonder racing again that she hadn't stopped to realize that she would be left behind.

Charlie and Jilly stood beside her on the drive. They would be leaving for the airport later that day to fly down. Jilly sensed what Ashleigh was feeling. "Don't worry," she said. "You know Terry and I will take good care of her."

"I know," Ashleigh said. Since it was impossible for Ashleigh to travel out-of-state during school, Terry Bush was taking over as Wonder's groom while Wonder was away from the farm.

"We'll call every night," Jilly added, "and Charlie can give you a progress report."

"She'll have plenty of eyes watching her," Charlie said.

Ashleigh had learned a long time ago that things didn't always go the way she wanted. She knew Wonder would be okay—she had three good and caring people with her. Ashleigh would be the one who would be miserable—left behind when all the important things were finally starting to happen to Wonder. For nearly three years, she'd spent part of every day with Wonder, and suddenly Wonder wouldn't be there!

Ashleigh tried to put aside her sad feelings, and spent the next few hours in Jilly's small apartment as Jilly packed for her stay in Florida. The two of them talked of the intense weeks ahead, leading up to Wonder's first race of the season. Charlie joined them for a few minutes before he and Jilly left for the airport.

"Get old Dominator out there on the trails while we're gone," he told Ashleigh. "I want the two of you in shape for when we get back."

Ashleigh knew he was trying to give her something to do to keep her thoughts and mind occupied. Dominator didn't really need the constant exercise to stay in shape, but she'd enjoy riding him anyway. She smiled. "I will."

"I'll keep in touch," Charlie said. "The filly's going to make us all proud."

As soon as they'd left, Ashleigh went back to the

house and called Linda. The stables suddenly seemed so empty.

"I know how you feel," Linda sympathized. "But, listen, we'll find things to do. I'll come over and ride with you—and you can come over here and help my Dad and me with our training. We could use a hand with the exercising. How about playing a couple of games of tennis with me after school? It's getting warm enough to use the outdoor courts."

"Sure," Ashleigh said, grinning, "if we wear a couple layers of sweaters. But yeah, I'd like to."

So, during the following week, Ashleigh stayed after school with Linda to use the school tennis courts. Ashleigh sure didn't have any reason to rush home, with Wonder gone.

Ashleigh spent a couple of nights at Linda's that week, too. They did their homework together in the evenings, and went out to help exercise the Marches' horses early in the morning before school. The March facilities weren't nearly as big as Townsend Acres, but the stable yard and training area were up-to-date and immaculate. It was pure joy for Ashleigh to be galloping a Thoroughbred around an oval again. She realized just how much she'd missed working Wonder on the track since Townsend had dropped her as a rider.

"I needed this," she told Linda as they rode off the track on two feisty three-year-old colts. Their cheeks were glowing from the sting of the cool morning air, and the horses' breath steamed mistily. "I think I'm going to be sore tonight. Breezing on the oval takes a lot more out of you than trail riding."

"Then you'll have to come over and help more often," Linda grinned. "My Dad sure appreciates it. He's shorthanded, and you want to be in perfect shape when you start breezing Wonder again."

"If that day ever comes," Ashleigh sighed.

"It will," Linda said with conviction.

There was one other thing Ashleigh and Linda did to fill the hours while Wonder was gone. They pored through the racing papers. Prep races for the Kentucky Derby were being run all over the country, and several horses were beginning to stand out from the crowd. Townsend Prince was one, but the West Coast had its own star, a black, finely bred colt named Mercy Man who'd just won the San Rafael at Santa Anita by ten lengths. Like Townsend Prince, Mercy Man was coming toward the Derby with a perfect win record.

"Wonder's the only filly seriously being pointed to the Triple Crown," Ashleigh said.

"Not too many fillies have ever won it," Linda agreed. "Not that that means anything."

But Ashleigh knew the odds of Wonder's joining their ranks weren't good. Not only were the Derby fields huge, with a tendency to become hectic jostling matches as horses and riders fought for positions, but colts were generally bigger and stronger. Fillies were given a concession in the weight they had to carry, but that wasn't always enough to even things out. It wouldn't be an easy race.

"The racing writers and handicappers aren't even mentioning Wonder so far," Ashleigh said.

"Well, she hasn't raced for a while." Linda frowned, then immediately brightened. "But if she wins the Swayle Stakes, they'll start talking about her, I'll bet!"

Charlie and Jilly called every night as promised. Charlie said Wonder had shipped well, and he liked the way she was taking to the track. "It's taken her a few days to get used to the heat, but so far so good," he said.

"I know she misses you," Jilly told Ashleigh when she got on the phone. "She looks over the stall door every time someone comes into the barn—as if she's expecting you. But don't worry. Terry and I are giving her so much attention, she'll be spoiled rotten before she gets home."

Ashleigh smiled, trying to visualize the scene Jilly described. But, oh, how she wished she were there!

On the morning of Wonder's race, Ashleigh called Linda and asked her to come over and wait with her for Charlie's call. None of the local television stations were doing live coverage of the race, so Ashleigh had no choice but to wait for Charlie's report.

"Gee, I can't, Ash," Linda said. "Seth's invited me to go to a folk concert with him this afternoon."

"He has?" Ashleigh was taken totally by surprise. She'd counted on Linda being with her. "You didn't say anything yesterday."

"He only called last night. I'm not really crazy about folk music, but it sounds like it might be fun. I'll keep my fingers crossed for Wonder, though."

Ashleigh hung up, feeling deflated and more alone than ever.

The Swayle Stakes was going off in mid-afternoon, and Ashleigh stayed in the kitchen to be close to the phone when it rang. Caroline buzzed through on her way out with Marcy.

"Why are you hanging around in here?" she asked Ashleigh. "It's such a beautiful day. You should go out and do something with Linda or somebody."

Ashleigh explained.

"Oh, right," Caroline said. "I forgot what day it was." Then she scowled for an instant. "It's funny—I can't believe Mike hasn't called you again."

"What's so funny about it?" Ashleigh said. "I didn't expect him to. I told you why he and Chad came by."

"Hmm," Caroline murmured, her forehead still furrowed. "Oh, well, I gotta go. See you later. Hope Wonder wins," she added over her shoulder as she rushed out the door.

Ashleigh alternately paced the kitchen and watched the minute hand on her watch move agonizingly slowly. She'd just about chewed her nails to the quick when the phone finally rang.

She grabbed up the receiver. "Hello, Charlie?"

"Yup. First chance I got to call. Terry's just taking her back to the barn. Wonder didn't win it, missy, but she ran a darn good race."

A wave of disappointment washed over Ashleigh. "She didn't win?"

"Don't sound so upset," Charlie said. "After coming off such a long layoff, I didn't expect her to win. The filly needed the race to get back in form. But she did come in second. Went right to lead and stayed there to the sixteenth pole, but a late-closing colt ran her down and just got his nose under the wire first. She put out too much too soon—set some incredible times. I've got to get Jilly to work at pacing her and saving some of her strength for the stretch. The filly wouldn't have tired if she hadn't sizzled so much through the first three-quarters. She'll have to run further than today in the Derby."

"Give her a kiss for me! When are you coming back?"

"Not sure. After the race today, Townsend was talking about sending her north for the Jim Beam at the end of the month. But I don't know. That's less than two weeks. I don't want to push her too hard. I'd rather wait for the Blue Grass in April. We'll see."

Wonder gone for another two weeks! Ashleigh thought. But

133

she tried to think of the good side. Wonder had run a good race; Charlie was happy—and Mr. Townsend must feel fairly confident in Wonder to even mention the Jim Beam. Then she had a thought. "If she runs in the Beam, she'll be running against Townsend Prince, won't she?" she asked Charlie.

"Maybe, but like I said, I'm going to try to talk Townsend out of it. If I run her in anything before the Blue Grass, I'd rather it be an allowance. We'll see."

Ashleigh hung up and hurried out to the breeding stables to tell her parents and Rory.

"Well, heck, second by a nose isn't bad," her father said. "It's pretty impressive, if you ask me."

Her mother agreed. "You can't be disappointed with that performance."

"Oh, I'm not," Ashleigh said quickly.

"When's she coming home?" Rory asked.

"Well, that's the bad news. Maybe not for a couple weeks."

Ashleigh left them and went up to the training stables. She knew a lot of the grooms were anxious to hear how the race had gone.

"I told Charlie all along the filly was good." Old Hank nodded. "But I think he's right about waiting for the Blue Grass. Don't want to push it."

As they were talking, Brad walked up the stable aisle and came over to them.

"So she ran well?" he said. When Ashleigh nodded,

she saw the barely disguised relief on his face. Wonder's good performance obviously took some of the sting away from Brad's having been responsible for her injury.

Ashleigh repeated what Charlie had told her. As excited as she was about Wonder's success, she couldn't help feel a coolness toward Brad, and her tone was cautious.

"She must have tired at the end," Brad said when she was finished. "And the field wasn't even that great."

Ashleigh bit back her irritation. "She was running against colts, remember, and she put out too much speed in the first three-quarters of a mile. Charlie wants to try and pace her in the next race."

"You said my father wants to put her in the Jim Beam?"

"That's what he told Charlie. But Charlie thinks racing her that soon would be pushing it."

"My father's right. She needs another race." Before Brad could say more, a feminine voice called to him. "Here you are, Brad. I thought you went to the office."

They all turned to see Melinda Westwood strolling toward them. She was dressed in expensive fawn riding breeches and gleaming leather boots. Her fair hair was ruffled from the wind. She and Brad had obviously been out riding. Melinda stopped beside Brad. She glanced at Ashleigh and Hank, decided they were only lowly staff, and turned her attention to Brad. "Ready to go?"

Ashleigh's irritation returned. "Isn't Prince running in the Beam?" she asked Brad with a taunt in her voice. "I'm surprised you want to run Wonder against him."

"There's no way Wonder could beat him," Brad laughed. "No one's expecting the filly to win if we enter her in the Derby. We're thinking of her breeding potential. If she runs a halfway decent race, it would up her value, and the value of her foals."

Brad's words were like a knife thrust, and he knew they hurt. He watched Ashleigh's face, waiting for her reaction, but Melinda had grown impatient. She laid a hand on Brad's arm. "We should really get going," she said. "We're supposed to be meeting my parents at the club in a couple of hours."

Brad turned and smiled at Melinda. "Sure. I'm finished here. Let's go." The two of them strode away.

Hank shook his head when they were gone. "Kid's got a lot of growing up to do. And if it comes down to his colt and your filly in the Derby, I'll put my money on the filly. That Townsend Prince may be a good horse, but he hasn't got the filly's heart."

As it turned out, Townsend Prince didn't run in the Jim Beam. The Townsends had decided to skip that race and concentrate on the Blue Grass at Kenneland in mid-April. The colt didn't have anything to prove. He'd won every race he'd been entered in. But Clay Townsend did press Charlie into running Wonder in the Beam.

Charlie was angry when he called Ashleigh with the news. "Nothing I can do about it. I don't like it, but she's in. It's going to take too much out of her, racing against such heavy competition so soon. There are three or four real good colts in the race—all headed for the Derby, all coming off good records. We just gotta hope for the best."

Again, Ashleigh waited anxiously, but this time at least the race was being televised, and Linda had come to watch with her. Caro came into the living room to watch, too.

"Figures Brad would take Townsend Prince out," Caro said. "He's probably afraid of Wonder."

"I doubt it, Caro," Ashleigh answered. "He doesn't think she can beat the Prince."

The race program began, and they all fell silent, eyes glued to the screen. Linda suddenly cried, "Look, there's Charlie and Wonder!"

Ashleigh had already seen. The commentators were reviewing some of the horses entered, and were showing clips of the horses before the race. The screen showed Wonder being led by Charlie from the saddling area.

"Unfortunately," the commentator said, "Townsend Prince, the colt everyone was hoping to see run today, isn't going to be here. But interestingly enough, his half sister is—Ashleigh's Wonder, a filly who had a late start, but raced well in the fall. She came back after a long winter layoff, due to injury, to run well in the Swayle Stakes. She's a definite long shot today — the only filly in this field of outstanding three-year-old colts, but she might hold some surprises. Her trainer, the respected Charlie Burke, seems to think so."

"How they'd ever get Charlie to say anything?" Linda said. "They must be making that part up."

The camera shot had changed again, and now focused on the horses as they went onto the track. "A field of ten for today's race, one of the major Derby preps . . ."

Ashleigh tuned out the commentator's voice and stared at the screen, watching for Wonder and Jilly. She felt her whole body tense with pre-race jitters as she finally saw them loading into the gate. The rest of the field looked good—too good. "You can do it," she whispered.

The gate doors flew open, and the race was on. Wonder was in the Number Five post position, but with the rush of horses surging out of the gate, Ashleigh had trouble spotting her. The camera angle didn't help. She listened to the announcer's call as he ran down the lineup of the field. Wonder and Jilly were laying third, on the outside, with two horses running inside them closer to the rail.

Ashleigh focused on Jilly's green-and-yellow silks. She saw them moving up along the outside. In a moment she had a clear view of them. She saw, too, that Jilly and Wonder were fighting a battle of wills. Jilly had Wonder in a tight hold as she desperately tried to pace the filly and keep her from going straight to the lead—running too fast, too soon. But Wonder wanted no part of being held back. She arched her neck in rebellion and managed to move up into second halfway down the backstretch. Ashleigh could see Wonder's frustration. The filly was breaking out in a sweat. "You'd better let her run, Jilly," she whispered.

Two of the favorites, Rhythmic and Nononsense, were starting to make their moves from the back of the pack. They were both late closers, whose style was to outrun the tiring speed horses in the stretch. The two were rapidly gaining ground. The third betting favorite, Jonpur, was running just ahead of Wonder, setting a blazing pace.

As the field neared the far turn, Ashleigh saw Jilly give up the battle of wills. She must have realized that holding the frustrated filly back was doing Wonder more harm than good. Ashleigh breathed a sigh of relief as Jilly let Wonder have rein. The filly shot forward as if she'd been propelled from a cannon. She came around the turn wide, but she was already showing the leader her heels.

"Go, Wonder," Ashleigh breathed. "You know you can do it."

"And Ashleigh's Wonder has taken the lead," the announcer called. "Nononsense and Rhythmic are making their moves. Nononsense is moving up along the rail. Rhythmic is putting in his drive on the outside. They've passed the rest of the field, but Ashleigh's Wonder, a long shot, is still holding on to a strong lead. And down the stretch they come! Rhythmic is gaining slightly on the outside. He's got a half-length edge on Nononsense, who's moving up on the rail. But they're not going to catch this filly! She's still pouring it on, and she's pulling away from these colts. With only a furlong to go, she's increased her lead to three lengths. Rhythmic and Nononsense are fighting for second, but they're no threat to this filly! She's under the wire, and Ashleigh's Wonder wins the Jim Beam by four lengths!"

Ashleigh bounded to her feet, dancing in excitement. "You did it, girl! That's the way!"

"What a race!" Linda cried, jumping up and giving Ashleigh a high five. "She put them away like they were broken-down claimers. I don't believe it!"

"That'll show Brad," Caroline gloated. "The Prince has got something to worry about now!"

Ashleigh listened ecstatically to the commentator's

words, ". . . a real upset today . . . a filly coming out of comparative obscurity . . . a resounding victory . . . and under a hand ride, too!"

The cameras followed Wonder and Jilly's progress to the winner's circle. Jilly was beaming. Soon Charlie and Clay Townsend joined them. But Ashleigh's eyes were on Wonder. The filly pranced and tossed her elegant head as Jilly dismounted, but Ashleigh noticed that Wonder's brilliant copper coat was absolutely bathed in sweat.

The program had no sooner ended than the phone rang. Caroline jumped up to get it. She returned a second later, her eyes dancing. "Ash, it's for you."

Ashleigh frowned, her mind still on the race. She picked up the phone in the kitchen and said a breathless hello.

"Hi, Ashleigh?" a male voice asked.

"Yes?"

"It's Mike Reese. I just saw the race. Congratulations! She was really impressive."

It took Ashleigh a second to pull her thoughts together. "It was pretty incredible, wasn't it? Thanks!"

"Couldn't happen to a better filly," Mike laughed. "Well, I just wanted to congratulate you. When's she coming back?"

"Soon, I hope. She's entered in the Blue Grass, though I haven't talked to Charlie yet. I don't know how she came out of the race."

"It's a tough campaign for any horse, but she definitely looked good. I'll talk to you soon."

Ashleigh was in a daze when she went back into the living room. She was really surprised Mike had called. But she couldn't get her mind off of Wonder's appearance after the race. Mike hadn't seemed to notice the filly's condition, but of course, he didn't know Wonder like Ashleigh did.

It took her a second to realize Caroline and Linda were both grinning at her—and only another second to realize why.

"He saw the race and wanted to congratulate Wonder," Ashleigh said shortly.

Caroline chuckled. "Sure. I wonder how many other people he calls when their horses win?" She winked broadly to Linda.

Ashleigh shook her head. "You guys are impossible!"

Charlie called a half hour later, and he didn't sound like the pleased trainer of a winning horse. "The filly's beat," he said. "She put too much into it. I made a big mistake telling Jilly to pace her. The filly got herself worked up into a real state because Jilly held her so long. The race didn't tire her—fighting with Jilly did. My fault."

"You didn't know. She's okay otherwise?"

"Yeah. She just needs a little rest. Doesn't look like

142

she's going to get it, though. Townsend told me after the race that he definitely wants to run her in the Blue Grass. Short of putting the filly out of commission myself, I don't know how I can change his mind. He doesn't see three big races in a month just before the Triple Crown campaign as a problem. He says the filly's only been lightly raced till now and had the whole winter off to rest. No darned good putting this much pressure on her, but he's the owner." Charlie growled with disgust. "At any rate, she did us proud. We'll be home day after tomorrow. She'll probably pick up faster in her home stable. The filly will be glad to see you."

"I'll be glad to see her, too!"

12

COREY HURRIED OVER TO ASHLEIGH AFTER FIRST PERIOD HIS-
tory class on Monday. "Hey, you sure made the papers this weekend!" Corey cried.

"Well, not me personally," Ashleigh laughed. The
Sunday papers had carried a big article about Wonder's success in the Jim Beam, and there'd been a color
photo of the horse, Charlie, Jilly, and Clay Townsend
in the winner's circle at Turfway. Even though Ashleigh knew Wonder had come out of the race tired,
reading the write-up had been one of the most thrilling moments in her life.

"Everybody's talking about it," Corey said. "They
know you've done most of the work with Wonder.
What did Brad have to say?" she added with a grin.

"I haven't seen him yet. He wasn't around the stable
yesterday."

"He was probably off with 'Miss' Westwood." Corey snorted.

"You're nuts," Ashleigh said with a laugh.

"So Wonder and Brad's horse will be running against each other in the Blue Grass, huh? My father bought advance tickets, but then almost everyone in Lexington goes to Keeneland that day."

"Yeah," Ashleigh sighed, suddenly feeling less cheerful. The papers had played up Wonder and Townsend Prince racing against each other. "Charlie and I don't like it. It's too many big races for her in too short a time."

"Come on, where's your fighting spirit?" Corey cried. "You've got to give Brad a run for his money. Oh, by the way," she added slyly, "I saw Mike Reese in town over the weekend. Did he ever call you?"

Ashleigh felt her face flushing. She wouldn't have reacted like that a few days before, but she was remembering Caroline and Linda's teasing about his call. Her expression was a dead giveaway.

"So he did!" Corey yelped. "Wait till Jennifer hears."

"Corey, don't—" Ashleigh began, but Corey was already sprinting off down the hall.

On Tuesday Charlie and Wonder returned home. Ashleigh rushed up to the stables after school to see Wonder leaning her elegant head out over her stall door. "You're home!" Ashleigh cried joyfully. The filly was just as thrilled to see Ashleigh. She whinnied and thrust her head against Ashleigh's shoulder when Ashleigh reached the stall.

"Oh, you gorgeous thing!" Ashleigh lovingly hugged the filly, then dropped a kiss on Wonder's nose. "I missed you so much! It's been so lonely around here, but you did such a great job. I'm so proud of you! You're a real fighter, girl."

Wonder grunted, in her own way telling Ashleigh how glad she was to be home again. Ashleigh let herself into the stall, and Wonder poked her velvet nose near Ashleigh's pocket, sniffing meaningfully. Chuckling, Ashleigh reached in her jacket and found a carrot. Then she stood back to get a better look at Wonder.

It took only a glance to see that the filly was thinner than usual. Ashleigh ran her hand over Wonder's rib cage and felt the slight indentations between each rib that hadn't been there before. She turned as she heard someone just outside the stall.

When she saw who it was, she smiled warmly. "Hi, Charlie! Welcome home."

Charlie nodded and smiled. "Guess you noticed she's lost some weight," he said.

"Is she off her feed?"

"That—and the races took a lot out of her. She gave it more than a hundred percent."

"But otherwise, she seems okay?" Ashleigh said, worried.

"I don't see any physical problems, but I haven't worked her at all. I just let her hang around in her stall a couple of days and take it easy. I thought we might take her out for a slow jog on the trails tomorrow." He scowled. "I'd rather give her a little more time off, but we can't afford to let her lose condition."

As they spoke, Terry and Hank walked up. "Glad to have her back?" Terry grinned to Ashleigh.

"I sure am."

"Don't worry, I took good care of her for you," Terry said.

"I can see that."

Hank had turned to Charlie. "She's put in a couple of good races. How you feeling about the Derby?"

Charlie shrugged. "Not sure, yet."

"That Townsend kid's been full of talk—telling everybody they don't expect the filly to win . . . that they're only putting her in to knock up her breeding value."

Charlie snorted his disgust. "Hope you had enough sense not to listen to him. His father's got more of an opinion of the filly than that."

"Did Jilly come back with you?" Ashleigh asked Charlie.

"Maddock's given her some more mounts down in Florida."

"Yeah," Terry put in, "and since the Beam, some other trainers have been talking to her."

"Hey, that's great for Jilly!" Ashleigh exclaimed.

Charlie cocked a shaggy, gray brow. "Yup. So it looks like you'll be working Wonder up until the Blue Grass."

"You mean it?" Ashleigh's face lit with excitement.

"Wouldn't say so if I didn't."

Townsend Prince, fit and looking good, arrived back at Townsend Acres the next day. From then on, Ashleigh ran into Brad more than she liked, at the morning workouts and inside the stables. He was incredibly cheerful—but why wouldn't he be? Townsend Prince was in perfect condition. He hadn't been overraced; his gallops on the oval were impressive. He looked like a sure winner in the Blue Grass, and his only threat in the Derby seemed to be the West Coast star, Mercy Man. Brad never said a word about Wonder's incredible performance in the Jim Beam, but it was obvious he still didn't consider her a threat. Townsend Prince and Mercy Man both greatly outclassed the horses she'd beaten.

The Saturday of the Blue Grass came too quickly. Ashleigh arrived at the beautifully manicured Keeneland track early in the morning with Charlie and Jilly. The previous day had been rainy and overcast, but that Saturday had dawned warm and sunny—a gorgeous spring day. Leaves were sprouting on the trees, and the grassy areas of the track were a brilliant green. Ashleigh was excited, but apprehensive, too. Wonder had been training well in the two weeks since she'd returned from Florida, but she hadn't regained all the weight she lost, and Charlie still felt she needed more time to rest.

He shook his head as he studied the rest of the field in the saddling area. "Townsend Prince is as fit as a fiddle," he said to Ashleigh. "A couple of these other horses haven't been raced in a month either. I don't like it," he grumbled.

"You don't think she can do it, then," Ashleigh said as she steadied Wonder so that Charlie could tighten the saddle girth.

"We both know she'll try her darnedest, but with that rain yesterday, the track's still heavy. It's drying, but it's sure not fast. Running in that'll take more out of her. And that Sandia's a real speed horse. I don't know if he's got any staying power, but if she tries to run on the lead like she usually does, she'll be running in a speed duel with him. They'll tire each other out and make it easy for Townsend Prince to take over in the stretch. Silverghost's a late closer, too, and they're both fresh horses. It's not going to be an easy race for our little lady."

Ashleigh glanced over at Wonder. The filly looked like she always did going into a race—alert and on her toes. But Ashleigh knew Charlie was right. The race

149

was going to be tough. And this was the worst possible time for Wonder to be going into a race tired—when she was facing Townsend Prince for the first time.

Ashleigh tried to keep her hopes up as she led Wonder into the walking ring. Spectators mobbed the area around the walking ring. Ashleigh saw Corey, Linda, and Jennifer push in close to the edge of the ring and wave. They were studying both Wonder and Townsend Prince. She saw other familiar faces, too. Knowing so many of her friends would be watching the race made winning even more important. She'd talked so much about Wonder. She wanted them to see firsthand just how good the filly was.

Then Charlie and Jilly joined her in the ring, and with last-minute instructions from Charlie, Jilly mounted. Jilly knew exactly what she and Wonder would be up against.

Ashleigh and Charlie took their places in the stands, and Ashleigh turned and waved back to Linda, who was sitting with her family. Then she turned her attention to the field.

Ashleigh had a premonition before the horses even left the gate that this wasn't going to be Wonder's day. But as the race began, she felt hope stirring again.

Sandia went right to the lead in the nine-horse field, with Wonder running just behind in a close second.

The rest of the field tapered out behind them, with Townsend Prince in a fast-closing fourth.

"If Jilly can keep her there, off the lead," Charlie said, "we just might have a chance she won't tire before the stretch."

Wonder and Sandia stayed in their positions right down the backstretch and into the far turn. Townsend Prince was remaining back in fourth on the outside, only a few lengths behind. But Sandia was setting terribly fast fractions, especially considering the heavy and tiring surface of the track.

Ashleigh saw Charlie shake his head somberly when he saw the times.

As the horses came off the turn into the stretch, Jilly let Wonder go. The filly valiantly dug in and moved up on Sandia, getting her nose in front of the colt, then her neck. But it didn't take an expert to see that Wonder was tiring, or to see that Sandia was struggling and tiring even more. They were losing their lead on the rest of the field. The fast early speed was taking its toll. And Townsend Prince was moving up rapidly on the outside, fresh and full of go. Silverghost was edging up on the rail. Sandia dropped back. Townsend Prince flew past him, then Silverghost followed. With only an eighth of a mile to go, Townsend Prince was gaining on Wonder with every stride.

The filly, as tired as she was, wasn't giving up. Ashleigh felt her heart swell with pride to see Wonder courageously fight on, struggling to keep her lead, digging in again, and again. But Wonder just didn't have enough left. At the sixteenth pole, Townsend Prince surged ahead and went under the wire to a length's victory. Silverghost had raced up on the tiring filly, too, to beat Wonder by the barest nose.

Ashleigh's eyes were stinging with tears as she and Charlie silently left the grandstand. Her tears weren't over Wonder's loss, but over the incredible effort Wonder had had to put out. The filly should never have been forced to run in the race to begin with!

"Pretty much what I expected," Charlie said glumly when they met Jilly and Wonder on the backside. Wonder's copper coat was lathered white, and she hung her head in exhaustion. "But you showed your heart again, little lady, didn't you?" he added as he stroked Wonder's wet neck. "If she hadn't put out so much in her last race—if she'd had more time to rest—she could have held on. This wouldn't have happened!"

Ashleigh took Wonder's reins as Charlie removed her saddle. She was so upset at Wonder's condition, she couldn't talk. She and Charlie immediately sponged the filly down, then Ashleigh walked her under the trees.

"Oh, girl, we put you through a lot today, didn't we?" she whispered. Wonder wickered tiredly. "But I'm so proud of you. You're such a fighter."

When Ashleigh led Wonder back to the stable, she saw an excited and congratulatory crowd gathered around Townsend Prince's stall. Brad and his father were there, and Melinda Westwood and her father, along with a dozen reporters. The gloating smile on Brad's face made Ashleigh feel sick.

Jilly joined them at the stall when Wonder was comfortably settled. Jilly had changed out of her jockey silks, but she was looking tired and discouraged, too. "The pace was too fast early on," she said. "And the track was lousy. Wonder put her heart into it. She just didn't have anything left against Townsend Prince."

"If she'd come into the race as fresh as he was, it might have been different," Charlie said with a touch of anger. "I'm not writing her off yet." He leaned against the stall wall and gave Wonder a careful scrutiny. "She's tired, but not in as bad shape as she might have been after that effort."

"She'll never be able to run in the Derby after this," Ashleigh said. "It wouldn't be worth it, if she had to burn herself out."

Charlie pulled down the brim of his hat and squinted thoughtfully. "We've got three weeks to get her in shape for the Derby, and we're going to make them count. They haven't seen the last of us yet."

"But how?" Ashleigh asked. "What she needs is more time to rest."

"People may say I'm crazy," Charlie answered, "but

I'm not going to work her at all for the next week. We'll take it easy and let her fatten up some. Then we'll take her out cross-country, build her up nice and slow. I'm not going to work her hard on the oval until a few days before the race. Then we'll get her out there, wake her up, and get her buzzing."

They brought Wonder home that night. Ashleigh was feeling slightly more hopeful after hearing Charlie's plan and knowing he hadn't given up. She hadn't given up either, but Wonder would be facing more than Townsend Prince in the Derby—she'd have some other fierce competition, too.

A phone call to Linda helped, too. Linda agreed that the loss wasn't Wonder's fault. When Ashleigh told Linda of Charlie's unusual plan, the other girl paused, thinking.

"Well, Ash, I'd have to trust Charlie. With the two of you taking care of her, I bet Wonder's going to snap back, one hundred percent."

The next morning at the breakfast table, Caroline picked up the Sunday sports pages. "Oh, God, look at this!" she snorted to Ashleigh. "Townsend Prince and Brad, and more Townsend Prince and Brad. How disgusting! You have *got* to beat him in the Derby, Ashleigh!" Caroline tossed the paper across the kitchen table, almost knocking over Rory's glass of juice.

"Caroline," Mrs. Griffen said, reaching for the glass,

"take it easy. They'd do the same for any horse who'd won."

"It's Brad's *attitude*."

Mrs. Griffen hid her smile.

"Wonder still did pretty good," Rory said between mouthfuls of cereal. "She came in third and beat all those other colts."

"But they hardly mention that," Caroline frowned.

Ashleigh had already skimmed most of the articles and had been pretty disappointed with the lack of praise for Wonder. Now Caroline grabbed back the paper. "Listen to this," she said as she read aloud, " 'Ashleigh's Wonder held up to a sizzling early pace, but tired badly in the stretch. It looks like she'll be outclassed by the field she'll meet in the Derby.' They're not giving her much credit, are they?"

"It's only words," Mr. Griffen said. "One reporter's opinion. But while we're on the subject, you do realize that she's going to be running against the best three-year-olds in the country? We're all expecting an awful lot of Wonder. I think we should be very happy to just see her run a good race."

There was a feeling of tense anticipation in the stables over the three next weeks. Everyone sensed it—two Townsend Acres horses running in the Derby. One was an almost sure favorite to win; the other was the favorite in the hearts of the staff. There was growing admiration among the stable hands for the courageous little filly, who sometimes seemed more of a pet than a member of the racing string.

That support helped Ashleigh through the tiring days. Each morning she was up at four and out to the stables for three hours' hard work before school. Then she was back to the stables after school, with the prospect of hours of homework to labor over after dinner. She knew her mother noticed her weariness, but for once Mrs. Griffen didn't say a word to Ashleigh about spreading herself too thin. All the Griffens wanted to see Wonder win the Derby. It had become a matter of family pride. The Kentucky Derby was a great American tradition, and this year they all had a stake in it!

Linda was as caught up in the pre-Derby excitement as Ashleigh. She'd also decided that she'd seen enough of Seth Hoffman. "He's nice as a friend and all," she told Ashleigh, "but when we go out on dates, he can be really boring."

Linda and Ashleigh brought newspaper clippings and copies of *The Daily Racing Form* to school and studied them over lunch. Even the papers that usually ignored horse racing had articles about Derby prospects.

"None of the field have got Wonder's times beat," Linda said, comparing the records of the various entrants. "Not one of them has run a mile in one-thirty-four. And she should be able to go the distance. . . ."

To Ashleigh's surprise, Corey and Jennifer had

taken a genuine interest, too, joining Ashleigh and Linda in their analysis. But Ashleigh was really astonished when kids she barely knew stopped to talk to her about the race.

"You're a celebrity!" Corey told her.

"Be serious," Ashleigh laughed.

"I am! Someone from our class has a horse in the Derby. How often does that happen?"

Not often, Ashleigh knew. She only hoped she and Wonder could live up to everyone's expectations.

Charlie had Ashleigh start working Wonder at an increasingly brisk gallop on the oval. The week of complete rest had worked miracles on the filly. She'd put some weight back on, and there was more energy in her step. The cross-country jogs had built up her stamina, and when Charlie finally put her back on the oval again, she wanted to run.

Ashleigh could feel the renewed power in the filly. And Ashleigh wasn't making any mistakes now. She was one with the horse beneath her—the two of them single-minded as they pounded over the dirt in the crisp morning air, with just the sounds of Wonder's steady hoofbeats and expelled breaths breaking the silence.

It helped, too, that Townsend Prince had already been shipped to Churchill Downs to work out there. Ashleigh didn't need the distraction of Brad's watching eyes, and Charlie was convinced that Wonder would condition better on her home ground, where she could relax away from the bustle of the track. He wasn't shipping the filly over until three days before the race, and although both Mr. Townsend and Ken Maddock questioned the wisdom of his decision, Charlie stuck to his guns.

On the day before Wonder was to be shipped, Ashleigh breezed her for the first time, pushing her through six furlongs, then galloping her without pressure for a mile and a half. Wonder came out of the gallop prancing and tossing her head—not the least bit tired.

Ashleigh laughed as she patted the filly's neck. "You're back in shape, girl. Ready to go!"

She rode Wonder off the oval, then stared in surprise to see Mike Reese standing beside Charlie. He gave her a big smile.

"She's looking good. Nice gallop," he called.

"What are you doing here?" Ashleigh blurted out.

Charlie answered for him. "I've been giving him and his friend some pointers. Told him to come over and watch."

"Oh," Ashleigh said.

"Charlie told me how he was bringing her back from her last race," Mike said as Ashleigh rode over to them and dismounted. "To be honest, I didn't think she'd come back that fast, but I see I was wrong."

"How'd she feel?" Charlie asked as he checked Wonder over.

"Absolutely great," Ashleigh said, but she could sense Mike watching her, and it made her uncomfortable.

Charlie straightened from checking Wonder's legs and readjusted his hat. "Like I said, they haven't seen the last of us yet. Give her a good long walk to cool her out," he added. "It's warmer than usual this morning."

Ashleigh nodded and started leading Wonder off.

"I'll see you at the Derby," Mike called after her. "In the winner's circle, I hope."

Ashleigh looked back and grinned. "Right!"

13

ASHLEIGH AND JILLY LEFT FOR CHURCHILL DOWNS BEFORE FIRST light to make the seventy-five-mile drive to Louisville. The rest of the Griffens would follow later on that morning. Even in the early hours before the admission gates were open, the track had a carnival atmosphere. Every hotel and motel in the area was booked, and every seat in the grandstand taken. Not only would racing fans be flocking to the track, but there would be celebrities galore, and spectators who never went to another race except for the Kentucky Derby, the first weekend in May.

Television camera crews were setting up their equipment on the backside as well as in the grandstand area. Reporters were already streaming through the stables and barns, seeking interviews. Ashleigh could feel the high pitch of excitement everywhere she turned. Only Charlie seemed to be able to ignore it and stay calm. He went about his business as if it were just a normal day, checking in on the filly, talking to the other trainers and Jilly, giving a few gruff interviews to reporters.

Ashleigh was in the stall, keeping Wonder company, and overheard some of the reporters' questions. "She's got early speed," one said to Charlie, "but what do you think of your outside post position? She's twelve in a field of fourteen. Won't that be a disadvantage?"

"I like it fine," Charlie said. "It'll keep her out of the crush on the rail."

"How do you feel about her being the only filly in the field?" another asked.

Charlie shrugged. "She's run against colts before. She's a good filly. She'll do her best."

"There's talk that she's been overraced—that she came out of the Blue Grass a pretty tired third."

"And beat eight colts and only lost by a length."

The reporter laughed. "Any second thoughts about putting Jilly Gordon up as jockey? I know she's ridden the filly all along, but she'll be up against the top jockeys in the country today—the only woman, too."

"Jilly knows how to handle the filly, and the filly likes her. That sounds like a good combination to me," Charlie said.

"What's your strategy for the race?"

"You'll see that when we're out on the track."

Ashleigh was surprised when another reporter, a

woman, looked in over the stall door and spoke to her. "Are you Ashleigh Griffen?" At Ashleigh's nod, she continued, "I've been hearing rumors from some of the grooms that you actually raised this filly and have been helping with her training."

"Well . . . yes."

The woman smiled. "What can you tell me about it? I'd like to hear."

Ashleigh didn't see any harm in talking to the reporter. Wonder's history certainly wasn't a secret. She quickly outlined the facts. The reporter listened with interest and jotted down some notes. Then she looked over at Wonder and smiled again. "Beautiful filly. I'll be rooting for the ladies today."

Ashleigh grinned and waved her off, and moments later Linda appeared. Linda and her family were only spectators at the Derby, but Linda couldn't resist coming to the backside.

"I wanted to come now before it got too crazy," Linda said. She was dressed in a blouse and a pretty floral skirt. Everyone dressed up for the Derby. Ashleigh had brought along a new outfit she'd bought with Caroline's help, and would change before the race. "You should see it out there!" Linda motioned toward the grandstand area. "Tons of people, and all kinds of concession stands, selling souvenirs and stuff. Wild. How're you feeling? Nervous?"

"I've been too busy to get nervous yet. And Wonder seems okay. There've been a lot of reporters by."

"I came past Townsend Prince's stall on my way here," Linda said. "They practically have it roped off to keep people away. I had a look at Mercy Man, too. I hate to say it, but he looks good—real tall—over sixteen hands. But that doesn't mean anything. Where's Jilly?"

"She and Charlie just took a walk. They want to talk about the race."

Rory came rushing up. He was wearing a navy blue sports jacket, and for a change his hair was neatly combed in place. Ashleigh didn't expect that would last long. "Hi, Ash," he called. "We just got here. Mom and Dad are coming. Boy, are there a lot of people, and there's a band playing. I didn't know it would be like this." He came to the stall door. At ten years old, he was tall enough now to look over. "Hey, Wonder. You're going to win today, aren't you?"

The horse nickered and stepped closer, looking for a treat.

"Sorry, I haven't got anything," Rory said.

Ashleigh fished out a carrot and gave it to him as her parents arrived. Ashleigh blinked in surprise. They looked absolutely gorgeous. Her father wore a tailored gray suit and tie, and her mother wore a silky rose-colored dress and a big picture hat. "Wow!" Ashleigh said.

Her parents both grinned. "You don't get to see us dressed up very often, do you? Don't you think you should change pretty soon yourself?" her mother said.

"Yeah," Ashleigh agreed. "I'll just wait until Charlie and Jilly get back. Is Caro here yet?"

"She and Justin and his brother were right behind us when we parked."

Charlie, Jilly, and Terry Bush wove their way through the crowd along the line of stalls. Charlie nodded hello to the Griffens and tipped his hat. Jilly was beginning to look a little tense, but she smiled. "I love your hat," she said to Mrs. Griffen.

"Thanks. How are you doing, Jilly? This will be quite a race for you, to say nothing of being the only woman."

"Yeah," Jilly grinned. "I've been getting plenty of questions from reporters. I can't say I'm feeling calm, but we'll be all right once we're out on the track, won't we, Wonder?" she called to the horse.

Wonder was enjoying the attention and was gazing alertly at the crowd outside her stall.

"We'll head out," Mr. Griffen said. "You people need a little peace and quiet right now. Good luck, everyone. We'll see you up in the grandstand."

Her parents blew Ashleigh a kiss. She smiled back.

"Can't I stay?" Rory pleaded. "I'd rather be here with Ashleigh."

"No," Mrs. Griffen said firmly. "There's enough commotion around here without you adding to it."

"I'd be quiet—no one would even know I was here!" Ashleigh chuckled, trying to imagine that.

"Absolutely not." Mr. Griffen motioned Rory forward. "There's plenty to see out by the grandstand. You won't be bored."

They all set off, and Ashleigh checked her watch. "As long as you're here," she said to Charlie, "I guess I'll go change."

The trainer nodded, and Ashleigh grabbed the bag with her change of clothes and headed to the bathroom.

"I'll wait till you get back," Linda called after her.

Ashleigh changed quickly and brushed out her hair. She glanced at herself in the small mirror above the sink and decided she looked okay, if not exactly like her normal self. She was starting to get a nervous, fluttery feeling in her stomach. Not much longer before the race.

The bustle, excitement, and the many camera crews around the stables didn't help calm her as she worked her way back to Wonder's stall.

"Hey," Linda said when she saw Ashleigh returning. "The suit looks great! It makes you look older . . . or something. I like it."

"Thanks. Caro helped me pick it out."

"I'd better go find my parents before the crowd gets

too bad," Linda added. "I'll look for you in the walking ring."

After Linda left, Ashleigh went into the stall to give
Wonder a once-over. Earlier, she'd given the filly the
most careful grooming of her life, and Wonder still
looked magnificent. Her copper coat gleamed; her long
mane and tail hung in silky strands. But Ashleigh saw
a few bits of straw clinging to Wonder's long legs, and
grabbed a brush.

Charlie shook his head when he saw her and
reached over the stall door to hand her an old shirt.
"Put that on before you ruin that new outfit of yours."

Ashleigh grinned. "I wasn't thinking. How much
longer before we go out to the saddling area?"

"Not long now. Better to keep her in the stall as
long as we can so she doesn't get too excited."

But they weren't finished with visitors yet. Ashleigh
heard Caroline's call. "Hi, Charlie, Terry. It's crazy
here today. How's Wonder? Where's Ashleigh?"

Ashleigh went to the front of the stall. "Here." Caroline was standing arm-in-arm with Justin, and Chad
and Mike were just behind them.

For an instant Ashleigh was startled. Mike had said
he would be at the race. She just hadn't expected him
to arrive with her sister.

Mike walked right over to the stall. "Hi. We're here
to cheer for you like we promised. How're you doing?
How's the filly?"

Ashleigh smiled nervously. "Fine."

"I'll be back in a minute," Charlie said. "Don't let that filly get too excited." Wonder came up to the stall door with ears pricked, studying the visitors. Ashleigh tried to think of something to say to Mike, but suddenly something else caught her full attention.

Brad and Melinda were walking along the line of stalls, and there was no way they could avoid Caroline and the others. *Oh, no,* Ashleigh thought. *How's Caroline going to react to this?*

But her sister surprised her. Caroline looked up, saw her ex-boyfriend and his new girlfriend approaching and gave a careless, casual wave. Caroline had her very good-looking new boyfriend standing at her side, which might have had something to do with it. But she also looked fantastic. She'd searched long and hard for the perfect outfit for the Derby. Ashleigh knew, because she'd been with her, and had had a booming headache before Caro had finally decided on a sleekly simple pale blue dress that matched her eyes. She'd found a swooping brimmed hat to match, and Caro's perfectionism had paid off.

Brad couldn't seem to take his eyes off Caro. "Hi, Caro," he said. "Here for the big day?" He suddenly seemed to remember the girl at his side. "I don't think you've met Melinda. Melinda, Caroline."

Either Caroline was an incredible actress, Ashleigh thought, or her sister really didn't care about Brad anymore. Caroline smiled warmly at Melinda. "Hi, nice to meet you. This is a good friend of mine, Justin McGowan, and his brother, Chad, and Mike Reese, whose family owns Whitebrook Farm. Looks like we're going to have a match race today after all," she said to Brad. "How's the Prince?"

Ashleigh couldn't help grinning in glee at her sister's performance. Melinda's eyes swept over Caroline, and she was obviously startled by Caroline's prettiness and sophisticated outfit.

Brad seemed impressed, too. He didn't resort to his usual put-downs of Wonder. "The race'll be interesting. The farm certainly has a lot going for it today."

"And may the best filly win," Caroline laughed.

"We'll see about that," Brad said with more of an edge in his voice.

As they moved off, Ashleigh saw Melinda furiously whispering to Brad —probably trying to find out who Caroline was. She doubted Brad would have told her about his ex-girlfriend. Ashleigh gave Caroline a wink and a grin of approval. Caroline smiled, understanding their silent communication.

"So that's Brad Townsend," Chad said. "I've never met him. Have you, Mike?"

"I've only seen him from a distance at the track and at auctions. We don't travel in the same circles . . . yet," Mike laughed.

"You think the filly can beat his horse?" Justin asked Ashleigh.

"Definitely—" Caro began, then let Ashleigh answer.

"If she can run up to her potential and doesn't get any tough breaks today," Ashleigh said seriously, "yes, I really think she can."

Mike gave her an admiring look, which Ashleigh tried to ignore. "That's the way to think," he said quietly.

Charlie came over and ended their conversation. "Time to break up the social gathering," he said. "The filly's got a race to run. Bring her out," he added to Ashleigh. "They're starting out to the saddling area."

"We'll see you in the stands," Caroline said. She came to the stall door and gave her sister an impulsive kiss. "Good luck," she whispered. "She can do it."

"I think so, too," Ashleigh whispered back. "Thanks, Caro."

Justin, Chad, and Mike echoed Caroline's wishes. Before they left, Mike caught Ashleigh's eye. "See you in the winner's circle," he said confidently.

Ashleigh hoped he was right. But from then on she didn't have time to think of anything but the race ahead. She brought Wonder out of the stall, and when Terry pointed to the old shirt covering her suit, she handed him Wonder's reins and quickly took it off.

Wonder had picked up on the excitement around

her. She knew she was racing—and she knew it was a *big* race. Her delicate nostrils were flared with anticipation as she pranced at the end of the lead shank.

Ashleigh glanced down the line of stalls and saw the same commotion going on outside Townsend Prince's stall. His groom was leading the Prince out, and Brad was right there, along with his father, Ken Maddock, Melinda, and some others Ashleigh didn't recognize.

Ashleigh tried to forget Townsend Prince. There were other good horses Wonder would be facing, like Mercy Man, and Sandia, and at least a half-dozen others who were coming into the race with good records and a chance of winning. There was always the possibility, too, of a long shot surprising everyone. Because she was the only filly, Wonder was considered a long shot, as far as the race analysts and bettors were concerned. An hour before race time, she'd been rated at thirty to one. Townsend Prince was almost even money to win.

"Keep her as quiet as you can," Charlie told Ashleigh as he led the way toward the saddling area.

Terry walked alongside carrying Wonder's tack as they followed Charlie. "I never thought I'd be here," he said.

"I hoped I would," Ashleigh answered as she gripped the lead and laid her other hand on Wonder's head, reassuring the filly. "But it's almost too much to believe, isn't it?"

"It sure is," Terry answered.

"Easy, girl," Ashleigh said as Wonder pranced sideways and strained against her lead. "It's a big race ahead, but you're going to win. You don't need to get too excited now."

The commotion in the saddling area was worse than in the barns. Crowds of spectators and media people surrounded the area. Track officials watched as each horse was tacked up by its trainer. It took all Ashleigh and Charlie's patience to keep Wonder calm until it was time for the horses to be led toward the walking ring by their grooms. "Just take it easy," Charlie said as he motioned Ashleigh off.

Ashleigh felt truly dazed as she led Wonder forward. She'd never faced crowds like this before! She recognized movie and TV stars. She saw network television cameras directed their way. Other cameras focused and snapped.

Even with her headgear and blinkers shielding her view, Wonder was startled by the crowds. She flung up her head, jerking on the lead shank.

"Easy," Ashleigh whispered. "Pretty soon you'll be out on the track and won't have to worry about them."

The filly snorted, listening, but she was tense and high strung, and Ashleigh's palms had gone clammy with sweat. But it *was* thrilling to be getting so much attention, and Wonder, seeming to know she was being admired, put on an elegant display of high spirits. She flared her nostrils, danced along on the tips of her toes over the thick grass, and swung her hindquarters out. Ashleigh had to work hard to keep her in hand.

Around and around they walked, over the lush grass of the walking ring. Then Ashleigh saw Charlie and Jilly and the other trainers and jockeys coming into the ring. It was time for the jockeys to mount and go out to the track.

Jilly looked pale but excited in her green-and-yellow racing silks. "I'm glad I don't have to ride in a race like this every day," she gasped.

"You'll do fine," Charlie said as he pulled down the stirrup irons.

"But there are so many people counting on me—you and Ashleigh and the Townsends," Jilly said. "The other jockeys won't let me forget it if I ride a bad race."

"You won't ride a bad race," Charlie scolded. "You haven't yet, have you? Once you get on the track, you'll forget all these jitters."

Jilly nodded grimly and tightened the chin strap on her helmet.

Ashleigh put her hand on Jilly's shoulder. "I know you'll do great. You know Wonder, and she trusts you. The two of you are going to try to win, and even if you don't, it's okay."

"Remember," Charlie said softly to Jilly, "you're going to be way on the outside. Get her out as fast as you can, but stay clear of the rat pack that's going to be fighting along the rail. She'll try to take you right to the lead. Let her. I'd rather take the chance of a fast early pace than have her get caught in behind horses. You're going to have Sandia and two or three others going right for the lead with you. You can try and pace her a little along the backstretch, but if you feel her fighting you, forget it. Just give it your best shot—that's all anyone can ask. You've got a good filly under you."

Jilly nodded in agreement. "There's no question of that, eh girl?"

Wonder threw up her head, and Charlie gave Jilly a leg into the saddle. Jilly picked up the reins, settled herself, and pulled her goggles in place.

Ashleigh took Wonder's head in her hands and kissed the filly's nose. "I believe in you, girl," she whispered. "I know you'll give it your all. Even if you don't win, we did it—we raced in the Kentucky Derby, and that's what matters!"

Wonder nickered and nudged Ashleigh with her nose. Ashleigh stepped back. "Good luck!" she said to both Wonder and Jilly.

Jilly smiled down at Ashleigh and Charlie, then patted Wonder's neck. "Okay, girl, let's go show 'em how it's done."

Jilly and Wonder moved off, following the line of Thoroughbreds and escort ponies already moving toward the passage under the grandstand that led to the track.

Charlie pushed back his hat, then grunted. "Can't do any more now but keep our fingers crossed."

14

CHARLIE AND ASHLEIGH QUICKLY THREADED THEIR WAY through the crowd. As they neared the grandstand, Ashleigh understood what the others had meant about the mob scene. People were everywhere, filling even the grassy infield of the track—noisy and boisterous, their cries blending with the bands that were playing.

Charlie and Ashleigh climbed the grandstand stairs. They passed beautifully dressed spectators holding racing programs and binoculars, who were staring out to the track as the horses began to come onto the field for the post parade.

Ashleigh felt her excitement building with every step. They soon found Ashleigh's family and the Marches halfway up the grandstand, with seats overlooking the finish line. Caroline, Justin, Chad, and Mike were just behind them. The Townsends were in more exclusive seats higher above them near the Stakes Room.

Ashleigh didn't mind that a bit. She didn't want to have to watch the race with Brad only a few feet away.

Everyone was smiling, and as soon as Ashleigh and Charlie had slid into the row, Mr. Griffen handed them each a pair of binoculars. Ashleigh didn't need them yet, but she immediately focused her eyes on the track and found Wonder and Jilly in the line of elegant Thoroughbreds circling in front of the grandstand.

Wonder pranced along at the end of the lead held by the rider of her escort pony. She arched her neck, and her rear feet danced beneath her muscular hindquarters. Otherwise, she showed no signs of excess nervousness. She was high-spirited, but not unruly, and she wasn't sweating at all.

"She looks good," Linda called over the noise in the stand. Ashleigh nodded and turned to Charlie. "What do you think?"

"So far, so good," the old trainer said.

Ashleigh studied some of the other horses in the field. Townsend Prince and Wonder were the only chestnuts, and the Prince, as usual, looked impressive —calm, alert, and in perfect condition. Sandia, a gray, seemed to be sweating up a little, but he wasn't fractious. Mercy Man looked impressive, too. He was easily the tallest horse in the field, and his muscles rippled under his gleaming black coat. He would run off the pace, Ashleigh knew, and his long stride would definitely be an asset in the stretch when he closed on tiring horses. Several other colts looked good. Wonder was definitely the smallest in the field, but Ashleigh told herself that Wonder had beaten bigger horses before.

Ashleigh hadn't really been listening to the commentary of the track announcer, but now the band struck up the chords of "My Old Kentucky Home," and the din in the stands quieted as everyone stood, singing the lyrics.

When the traditional Derby theme ended, the horses began their jog to the starting gate. Wonder still looked good, moving smoothly and comfortably. She seemed momentarily distracted by the crowd in the infield, but Jilly soon had her in hand. The horses approached the gate. Wonder would be one of the last to load. Jilly pulled her up well back from the gate and circled her at a walk as they waited.

The first five horses loaded in without trouble. Townsend Prince was one of them. The next two had to be coaxed and prodded. Sandia went in and Mercy Man. Two more horses loaded, then it was Wonder's turn. Jilly walked her to the gate. The filly seemed to be quivering with excitement, but she went in smoothly. The next horse, however, balked and reared, wasting seconds and giving the horses already loaded time to get fidgety. Finally he went in, and the last of the fourteen-horse field was loaded.

Ashleigh had her binoculars to her eyes. She was so tense, she could hardly breathe. She felt a hand squeeze her shoulder from behind and knew it was Caroline cheering her on. A dead silence fell over the track. Then the gate doors swung open with the ringing of bells, and the Kentucky Derby was off!

A wall of galloping horses surged onto the track. Those closest to the rail fought for position. Sandia went right to the front, followed by two other speed horses. Townsend Prince was just after them in fifth, in a good position for a later move. The rest of the field was bunched behind in a thundering mass of bodies. Mercy Man stayed back, clear of the congestion, and Wonder, on the outside, had clear running room, too.

Jilly was holding Wonder wide, close to the center of the track as the horses swept under the finish line for the first time.

"Good," Charlie grunted.

"As expected," the announcer cried, "Sandia's gone right to the lead and is holding it by a half. Jonpur is just behind in second, with Dr. Casey third along the rail. Sandia's setting a burning pace—the first quarter in twenty-two. Now Ashleigh's Wonder is moving up to challenge on the outside. Just behind her, Townsend Prince, in good position, then Nononsense in sixth, followed by Gyro, Break the Bank, Rhythmic, racing in a tight pack, and behind them on the outside, Mercy Man, who's running well off the pace as usual. Four lengths further back are Wanderkill and Jazz Beat, with Strawberry Fields and Silverghost bringing up the rear."

As the horses moved around the clubhouse turn, Ashleigh could see Jilly was trying to hold Wonder back in third. But as Wonder'd done before, she was fighting the restraint. They passed the half-mile pole.

"The half in forty-four flat," the announcer yelled. "Sandia still setting this bristling pace. They're into the backstretch. Dr. Casey is falling back now. Jonpur is fighting alongside him. Break the Bank is moving up on the rail, and Ashleigh's Wonder is challenging from the outside. She's moved into third under a tight hold by her jockey. Townsend Prince is moving easily in fourth, not ready to make his move . . . and here comes Mercy Man, getting into gear and moving up quickly on the outside!"

Ashleigh only had eyes for Wonder. "Don't use it all up," she whispered hoarsely. "You've got a long way to go!"

Ashleigh watched in agony as Townsend Prince began to slowly gain on Wonder. "No!" she groaned.

"Wait," Charlie muttered. "Jilly hasn't let her out all the way. The filly's got more."

Townsend Prince looked strong, with untapped reserves, and Mercy Man was now up in fifth.

The field swept into the far turn. "Let her go!" Charlie growled. Jilly seemed to be reading Charlie's mind, and dropped her hands, letting Wonder take the reins. Wonder shot into first coming around the turn, passing the tiring Sandia and Jonpur, but Townsend Prince was just behind her. Break the Bank was still gaining along the rail, followed by Silverghost and Rhythmic, who were also making late moves. Mercy Man was gaining rapidly on the far outside.

"And they're into the stretch!" the announcer shouted. "Ashleigh's Wonder has been asked for more and she's giving it. This is a hand ride! Her jockey's not carrying a whip! Sandia's dropped out of it, and Townsend Prince is gaining ground. He's in second, a half-length in front of Break the Bank, followed by Rhythmic and Silverghost going neck and neck. And Mercy Man is into his run and coming on strong!"

Ashleigh's ears were ringing from the screams of her family and friends, urging Wonder on. Charlie was nearly beside himself with excitement. "Don't give up now, little lady! Show 'em your heart!"

The other jockeys had long since gone for their whips. Jilly didn't have that option. She kneaded her hands along Wonder's neck, asking the filly for just a little bit more. And Wonder had it!

The filly dug in and showed the crowd every ounce

of her courageous heart. With two furlongs to go, she increased her lead to two lengths. But Townsend Prince wasn't finished yet, and he began moving up again to challenge. Mercy Man was gaining on his outside. But with less than a sixteenth of a mile to go, Wonder was holding the lead—not giving up an inch. The crowd was going wild.

Charlie had torn off his hat and was slapping it against his hand.

"Go, baby, go!" Ashleigh screamed.

The track announcer was nearly losing his voice in his excitement. "Townsend Prince and Mercy Man have moved up to challenge, but Ashleigh's Wonder is holding on by a half . . . now three-quarters . . . now a length! Townsend Prince and Mercy Man are running nose and nose, straining to catch her. What a finish! Can the filly do it? Can this courageous little filly hold them off? They're coming down to the wire —and I think she's going to do it! She *has* done it! Ladies and gentlemen, Ashleigh's Wonder has won the Kentucky Derby! What a performance! And with Jilly Gordon in the saddle! What a day for the ladies!"

Ashleigh was engulfed with hugs and kisses—her parents, Rory, Caro, Linda—even Charlie forgot his reserve for minute and gave Ashleigh a squeeze. "We did it, missy! We did it!"

Ashleigh knew she was laughing, yet there were tears streaming down her cheeks. How she'd dreamed of this day—had it really come true? She knew it had when Charlie grabbed her arm.

"Let's go," Charlie said. "They're waiting for us in the winner's circle!"

Ashleigh turned and saw Mike grinning down at her. "I told you," he called.

"Yeah," Ashleigh beamed back at him with incredible joy.

Ashleigh and Charlie filed out, down the grandstand steps, with the others following. People turned to stare, as if suddenly realizing this group was connected with the brilliant filly who'd won the race. Reporters had already spotted Charlie and rushed over as they worked their way through the crowd to the winner's circle.

"What are your reactions?" one asked.

"My reactions?" Charlie snorted. "I'm thrilled to death."

"You're not surprised by the outcome, then?"

"Told you guys all along the filly could do it."

"It must be a shock to the Townsend establishment —the filly beating her own half brother, who's undefeated until now."

"Later," Charlie said, waving the reporters away. "I've got a filly to congratulate."

The Townsends were already standing in the white-fenced enclosure of the winner's circle as the crowd divided to let Charlie and Ashleigh in. Clay Townsend hurried over to meet them. The normally businesslike owner was beaming. "You two belong in the winner's circle today. I never seriously thought she could do it, but I obviously was wrong. Incredible race—and what a day for the farm—first and second in the Derby!"

Behind him, Ashleigh saw Brad. Brad was the only one who wasn't smiling. His face was white and set. Melinda clung to his arm, and she seemed as stunned as Brad.

Ashleigh gazed past them to Jilly, sitting tall in Wonder's saddle, looking like she was going to faint from happiness. And there was Wonder, standing so proudly, with her head high and the thick blanket of red roses draped over her shoulders. The beautiful filly looked every inch a regal champion!

Then Wonder saw Ashleigh and whinnied.

Ashleigh didn't even think of the cameras focused on her as she ran forward and threw her arms around the filly's neck. Wonder dropped her head and lovingly nuzzled Ashleigh's shoulder.

"What a shot!" somebody cried.

Ashleigh wasn't listening. She was whispering words of praise in Wonder's ear. "You're amazing . . . I'm so proud of you . . . you showed them, didn't you? Oh, girl, I love you so much!" Wonder grunted at the praise and gently nuzzled Ashleigh again.

In a moment, Ashleigh looked up to Jilly. "You did an incredible job!"

Jilly's blue eyes were bright. "I'm so excited, I can hardly talk. I can't believe I'm sitting here in the winner's circle at the Kentucky Derby! And I don't even have my full jockey's license yet! Ashleigh, she ran the best she's ever run. She just kept giving and giving. She's amazing!"

Ashleigh turned back to Wonder and rubbed her velvet nose. "I know."

Someone hurried over with a microphone in hand. It was the woman who'd interviewed Ashleigh at the stable. "And here we have the trio of ladies who helped make this such an exciting day. You heard a part of their story earlier—the sickly filly, the girl who saved her and raised her, and the apprentice who's just become the first woman jockey to win the Derby! A perfect ending to a perfect day, if you ask me!"

Other newscasters swarmed around as Mr. Townsend and Charlie joined them before the presentation of the Derby trophy.

"What are your plans for the filly now?" they asked.

Mr. Townsend didn't hesitate. "Well, she's just won the Derby in nearly record time, under a hand ride, beating the best colts in the country, including one of my own. We can't very well bypass the Preakness and the Belmont after this performance. Look for us there."

Ashleigh turned to Wonder. "Did you hear that, girl? You're in the big time now!"

Wonder threw up her elegant, sculpted head, eyed the crowd, and gave a piercing whinny of victory.